A Game of Soldiers

'You're disgusting,' said Sarah. 'You want to see a doctor. You're sick.'

'Look,' said Michael in a voice of sweet reason. 'Either way he dies. How long does a sheep last, even, if it gets sick up there? He hasn't got a fur coat, Sarah, he's a man.'

Sarah rounded on him furiously.

'Yes,' she shouted. 'He's a man! A human being! And what are you saying – we've got to kill him! You're crazy, Michael. You're disgusting.'

Michael, Sarah and Thomas were tired of this war. Not that they saw much of it; their lives had just become more restricted and boring.

Sometimes, to pass the time, they'd pretend to find an enemy soldier and make him a prisoner of war. They could do their patriotic duty, like everybody else!

But where did the fun and games stop and the real war begin?

Jan Needle

A Game
of Soldiers

Fontana Lions

First published in Fontana Lions 1985
by William Collins Sons & Co Ltd
8 Grafton Street, London W1

Copyright © Jan Needle 1985

Printed in Great Britain by
William Collins Sons & Co Ltd, Glasgow

For Rod and Hilary

Chapter One

The night the soldier came, all three of them had been woken by the sounds of war. All three of them had lain in bed and listened to the noise of battle, and watched the uneasy flickering of lights in the sky. All three of them had been afraid.

It's getting nearer, Michael thought, and he slid his hand under his pillow to feel the wooden handle of the knife he kept there. It was a sharp knife – real blade-steel, not stainless that would never keep its edge, his father said – and it was curved, with a vicious point. It would kill a man, it would easily kill a man.

Michael held it on his bare stomach, under his pyjama jacket, and felt the cold wood and steel warming to his body. Pity it was French, that wasn't right somehow. It should have been British steel, Sheffield steel, the best. But this knife was the biggest his parents would allow, and in that size there had not been a British one for sale. In the matter of weaponry, naturally, patriotism came second.

He wondered if his father would regret it if the enemy came that night, to the house, and he – Michael – were slaughtered because his knife was not big enough to save him. He smiled at the thought. The knife he ought to have was black-handled, and wicked, with a six-inch blade at least. A commando knife. That would see them off.

His vision – of the pyjama-clad boy straddling a bleeding corpse in triumph – was frightened from his mind by a shattering bang that was the closest ever. Suddenly, his bedroom wall was illuminated as if by a lightning flash. In the intense whiteness a British marine surged forward from the poster, all white teeth and rifle. As it faded, Michael discovered to his shame that he was whimpering.

The shell, or bomb, or missile that switched Michael's brain from bloodthirsty fantasy to fright was the one which decided Sarah. As the crash came and the light intensified then died outside her curtains, she pulled back the covers and stood up.

She looked like a ghost in her long white nightie, she imagined. At least she felt like one, and she had a horrible certainty that soon she would be one in reality. Before she moved there was a series of further crashing explosions, and the shocking, short-lived roar of jets. It sounded as if a battle was going on quite near their house. Very near. Maybe her Mum and Dad were up already, getting ready to make a last desperate stand. As she opened her bedroom door, her mouth was dry.

But no. No lights were on, not even in their room. The door was open a little, though, which made her glad. They would have done that on purpose, in case she was frightened in the night. They would not mind her coming in.

'Mum? Dad?'

She called out softly so as not to wake them, just in case. She moved softly to their bedside on bare feet.

'Good God,' said Dad. 'It's the woman in white. Have you got an owl in your pocket?'

'You what?' said Sarah. A grin was on her face already. Impossible to stay afraid, or serious, with Dad. He was cracked.

'Florence Nightingale,' said her father. 'You won't know this, you ignorant bum, but she always carried an owl in her pocket wherever she went. See, I'm not the only nutter in existence.'

'She was the lady with the lamp,' put in Sarah's mother. 'The woman in white was in a book. Who was it by, now? Someone with a really funny name.'

'Look, don't mind me you two,' said Sarah. 'I'm only your little daughter standing here freezing to death. I'm only shaking with terror because we're all going to be murdered in our beds.'

'Oh, dare-dare diddums,' said Dad. 'Is the nasty mens keeping you awake with the naughty gunsiwunsies, den?'

'Yes,' said Sarah. 'I'm frightened.'

'Join the club,' said Mum. She shifted sideways so there was a gap between her and her husband, and pulled the covers back.

'Come on board,' she said. 'It may not be much but it's home. And there's always room for a littl'un.'

Thomas Wyatt had been awake for ages. In fact he had been awake for most of the night, long before the battle had flared up.

Many of Thomas's nights were broken, now. When he did sleep he often dreamed of war, and death, and blood and fire. In his most vivid and appalling dream, he was taken captive by some soldiers. After he had been held for some time his parents came for him. He tried to stand up, to run to them, but he never could, he could not move. And when they finally saw him, they turned away. In some dreams, he could still not move, or speak. But on the worst nights, he cried out then, in his nightmare, and called his mother. Both parents turned and looked again, then walked away. They did not *recognize* him.

When this battle had started, half an hour ago, Thomas had been lying on his back, staring at the ceiling. He had not been worrying about the dangers of the war, strangely, but about his best mates, Terry and

Joe. He had not seen them for a long time, well over a week, and he was missing them. He was certain that if the war went on much longer, if the school was not reopened, if no one could get about and visit town and so on – they would have forgotten him. Then he would be stuck.

The only friends Thomas had now were Michael, over at Tabb Hollow, and Sarah, who lived further still, about a mile or more. In the normal run of things, they had not been proper mates for ages, just neighbours. They had played together when they'd all been younger, when Thomas had been just a baby, but since then they'd got their separate friends.

Sometimes, like in the school holidays or when they were all at a loose end, they still got together, but it was quite an edgy thing. He was too old for Sarah to play mums and babies with him any longer, and neither of them got on all that well with Michael, who tried to be a bully. What's more, he only wanted to play at one thing these days, the one thing Thomas and Sarah disliked most. The war.

As he lay there, cuddling Red Bear and wishing he could go to sleep, the dominating noise was the wind. It was blowing quite hard, as usual, and it was shaking the roof and rattling the window in its frame. Thomas's nose, outside the covers, was cold. That was another thing: it was almost winter. Nothing was ever much fun in winter, here. This winter looked like being ten thousand times worse.

The battle started with quite terrifying suddenness. One second it was the desolate whining of the wind, the next a double roar of jet engines followed instantly by gunfire and the scream of missiles. Right from the start it sounded closer than ever before, and even under the blankets Thomas could see flashes, he was sure.

'Make them stop it, Red Bear,' he said, over and over

10

again, into the soft nylon fur of his bear-friend's stomach. 'Please make them stop it.'

For two minutes after the whimpering fit, Michael actually hid under his bedclothes, until shame at his cowardice brought him out. The handle of his knife was slippery – not with the blood of some dead foreigner, but with sweat. Michael forced himself to stand, and to go to his bedroom window.

At first there was little to see. It was a dark night, with running clouds and not much of a moon. He could make out the closer moorland, with the grass flattened and undulating in the wind. In the yard, his father's old van was rocking in the gusts, sometimes violently. There were few stars visible.

Then, straight ahead of him, the sky was alight with flashes. After a moment, Michael heard the detonations, and the buzzing, angry whines. Then there were jet engines, then a heavier thudding. Bombs, I bet, he thought. Give them hell! He paused. Give who hell? How the hell did he know who was bombing whom? And who was winning? Nobody told you anything, anymore.

He was depressed. All this was close. Any time, it could get closer. What if the house *was* overrun? What if they *did* come? What would happen?

Worse, would anybody know? Or care?

Michael opened the blade of his knife and put it close to his face. He stared at it, getting strength and courage, as if it were magic, a talisman.

Yes, they would know, and care. The British were here to save them, and they would, in due course. If anything *did* go wrong . . . they would also avenge.

Sarah lay between her parents' warm bodies, comforted but still afraid. Her father was asleep again. Genuinely,

11

she guessed, not just putting on an act to reassure her. He was breathing softly and evenly, his large chest expanding and contracting under his working shirt. Her mother was not asleep. But the conversation was over.

Both of them had petted her, and told her not to worry, and told her that everything would be all right, but she could not pin them *down*, that's what frustrated her. She wanted to *know*, she wanted to hear the details, to learn what they *felt* about the dangers. But that was not their way.

'Listen, you bum,' her Dad had said. 'Don't you worry your ugly little head about it. It's all in hand. I've given my men their instructions, and they're carrying them out. This noisy stuff is a diversion – I organized a fireworks display to keep the boys happy. You know what children soldiers are.'

He usually called her a bum, or something less polite, and he always called her ugly, and lazy, and a savage and so on. She loved his jokiness, and his niceness. But sometimes it did not help. She wanted an opinion. A straight, serious, honest opinion.

'There's no chance,' said her mother, when Dad had turned over for sleep. 'He'd be joking as they took him to the gallows, your Dad. That's why I married him.'

Sarah sighed.

'All right, *you* then,' she said. 'What do *you* think will happen?'

'Oh give up, Sarah,' replied her Mum. 'The best thing you can do is take his advice, isn't it? Don't *worry*.'

Hhm, thought Sarah. That was the trouble with getting on with your Mum and Dad. You couldn't even scream at them . . .

Listening to the guns, the bombs, the wind, the quiet rhythmic breathing . . . she went to sleep.

Thomas, unable to stand it any more, was out of his bed

and down the passageway. The house was small, only the two rooms upstairs plus the bathroom, and the last explosion had almost blown him to his parents' door, it had been so close.

Thomas had called out, twice, but not loudly enough for anyone to hear. If he had woken up his father, or even been heard, he would have been in trouble. That was not allowed. He'd called the first time with his head beneath the covers.

'Mum. Mum. Mum.'

Then had come louder bangs and crashes. Whiter flickerings.

His head outside the blankets, Red Bear clutched to his neck, he had wailed: 'Mummm. Muuum.'

Softly.

Outside their door, the last salvo still echoing like thunder in his mind, Thomas had whispered: 'Mum. Mum. Mum.'

There was a light on in there, and he could hear them talking. Very carefully, trying not to make a sound, Thomas sat down, so that the small bar of light shone dimly on his pyjama trousers. Very carefully he rested his head against the door, his back against the jamb. The voices murmured on. He liked that. They were talking.

What about though? He heard odd phrases clearly, then the rest was a mumble. It was about the war, of course. About this battle. He heard the word 'close' used several times, and he heard something about Foster's Landing, and Mr Gregory, a man he did not like. Thomas's father drank with Mr Gregory sometimes, and it could cause violent trouble. He had been hit once, by his father, when the men had had a jaunt. Hit very hard, and laughed at, and left crying in a field.

Thomas cuddled the bear that he had not bothered

with for more than a year until the war had come, cuddled the bear he could tell his private thoughts to and who listened. He found it comforting, like the murmurs through the door and the crack of light. In a few minutes, he was half asleep.

When the next burst of explosions came, Thomas came to with a jerk. Before he could stop himself he had shouted.

'Mum! Mum!'

Panic stricken, he scrambled to his feet. From inside the bedroom he heard the squeak of springs. Gripping Red Bear by the leg, he scurried quietly back towards his own door.

His father's voice came, loud, angry.

'Thomas! If you're outside here!'

As he scuttled into his room, he heard his parents' door jerked open. He stood against the cold bedroom wall, trying to pant without a sound. It was half a minute before the other door was closed and he could burrow back in between the blankets.

The soldier was in a ditch. It was very wet, but its deepness protected him from the wind. As he moved jerkily along, his helmet kept falling off, until he left it where it lay.

He was in great pain, and occasionally he was moaning, a sound that was lost in the ripping gusts that tore over his head and breathed coldly on him from around the grassy hummocks. From time to time he stopped moving and lay still. Gingerly he would feel the wound in his thigh. Deep, and wet, and bony. It filled him with terror.

The soldier did not know where he was, or even how he had got there. The battle had been confused, and he had been cut off from his comrades hours before. Of the moment he was hit, he remembered only a flash, an ear-shattering bang. Then nothing for a long long time. He guessed it was a shrapnel wound, the wound he could feel. He feared there were others, that he had not yet discovered. He was stricken with fear that he would die.

At the end of the ditch, in the darkness, the soldier put out his hand and touched something soft and strange. Almost before he had time to react, a distant shellburst lit up the sky. The soldier stared into a grinning, face-like thing, of gleaming white jagged bone, of teeth, of blood.

He opened his mouth to cry out, but nothing came. A longer flicker of high-explosive illuminated the broken body of a sheep.

Using his rifle as a stick, he pushed himself out from the shelter of the ditch to traverse the moorland in the freezing wind. He must find proper shelter.

A hiding place.

Chapter Two

By morning, the battle was over. In all three houses the families talked about it, and wondered.

Sarah's father switched off the radio with a grin. He had tried all the stations and got nothing. Even the English voices had made no mention of the battle. It was as if it had never happened.

'Somebody once said,' he told Sarah, 'that truth is the first casualty of war. One way of avoiding downright lies is to say absolutely nothing.'

'Three wise monkey principle,' said her mother. 'See no evil, hear no evil, speak no evil.'

Sarah, her breakfast finished, was standing at the window. The day was sunny, the sky a lovely blue, with racing white clouds. It looked cold.

'There aren't any wrecked planes,' she said. 'No sign of an army, no tanks. Maybe the radio's right. Maybe we dreamed it.'

In Thomas Wyatt's house, there was an argument going on.

'But I said I'd meet Sarah and Michael,' he was whining. 'I *said*. If I'm not there they'll ... they'll ...'

'They'll do sod all, Thomas,' his father said. 'What could they do? They'll just go away and play on their own.'

Thomas poked at his breakfast with his spoon. He was tired, and unhappy. Michael was nasty enough as it was. If he let them down this time ...

'But they'll be waiting,' he said. 'They'll freeze.'

His mother checked her husband's face to see how bad his mood was. The signs were not too awful.

'Oh let him go,' she said. 'I couldn't stand to have him inside all day, underneath my feet. And there was nothing on the radio. It can't've been that bad.'

Mr Wyatt snorted his contempt.

'Bloody pack of lies,' he said. 'What do they care? They wouldn't tell us if we had ten minutes to pack up and run. Bastards.'

Thomas looked from one face to the other. His parents' conversations about the war baffled him. He could not work out at this moment which side his father meant. Surely not the British?

'Well anyway,' said his mother. 'No point in worrying. The noise is over, and we're still here to see another day through. Let the lad go out to play. They can't be that close.'

'They can be that close,' snapped his father. 'They might be just over the ridge for all we know. What if he goes to play and he walks right into them, eh? That'd wipe the smile off, eh?'

Mrs Wyatt was not smiling. Nor was Thomas. He was terrified.

'Leave him be, Jim,' said his mother. 'Don't scare the kid.'

She turned to him.

'You won't go far, will you, Thomas? Stay close, all right? Just in case. And make sure that that Sarah looks after you.'

Thomas Wyatt nodded. He did not want to go.

Michael's parents did not appear much bothered either way. His father was preoccupied with the carburettor of the Land Rover, pieces of which were spread all over the kitchen table. His mother he had only seen for fifteen seconds. She had plonked a teapot down in front of him and gone to the wash house.

'Sounded like a big fight last night,' said Michael, tentatively. 'It sounded close.'

'Look at that,' said his father. He poked gently into the carburettor with a piece of wire. 'Why is it it's always the bit you can't get to? Sod's Law.'

Michael put some jam on another piece of bread. The clock ticking noisily on the window sill showed that it was almost time to go. He had a good plan. He was going to frighten Sarah.

'Do you think it was close, Dad? It woke me up.'

His father glanced up, surprised.

'Did it, son? You can't be working hard enough, then. It's almost time they got it over with, so you can get back to school. I'm surprised it's taking so long.'

This sounded hopeful. Michael liked it when his Dad talked about the war. He'd been in the army once, before he'd emigrated, and he knew all about it, and the equipment both sides had and all that. He'd said from the very start that it would be a pushover if only the Brits could get the men and gear down, and he sometimes talked about the enemy with great passion and hatred. Scum, he said, useless scum. But today he wasn't in the mood.

'Why *is* it taking so long, Dad? You said last week—'

His father put down the wire and took a mouthful of tea.

'Never you mind what I said last week, you just get out from under. I'm busy, your mother's busy, and I'm not going to sit and chatter.'

With a flutter in his stomach, Michael asked a silly question.

'If they're that close, Dad – shouldn't I take a shotgun with me? I mean, if—'

Michael's father had an odd face, long and smooth,

with very few whiskers and protruding eyes. These eyes held Michael's for a second or two, in a way that made him stop. Then his father made a kind of barking noise, a brief shout of laughter.

'Shotgun!' he said. 'You've got guns on the brain. You can have a shotgun for protection when your mother asks for one. She's working in the outhouse, all alone, without so much as a wooden spoon.'

Michael blushed faintly.

'And God help any soldiers that try to get the best of *her*.'

His father grinned.

'She'd eat them raw, son. And spit out the pips.'

The soldier, damp and violently cold, made it to shelter as the sun was rising. A stone shelter, with no roof, empty save for rocks and sheep droppings. As he crawled through the entrance and the wind was cut off, he almost wept with relief at the rise in temperature. He lay for minutes with his face on the earth, resting. For the moment he had no pain, he was numb perhaps. His fingers as he reached for his tin of cigarettes were white.

One cigarette left. Water rolled down his nose and almost wetted it. He struck four matches from his tin before he could hold one steady enough to light the cigarette. Plenty of matches, though. One cigarette.

The soldier lay on his side to smoke it, aware of the sun beginning to warm his legs through the door gap. He would save half of it, and warm his body in the sun until he had the strength to move further into the shelter. He would find a corner spot, safe from ambush, where he could command the door.

Then what?

He was wounded. He had no food. He had little water. Only half a cigarette.

There was a sharp pain as it burnt the soldier's lips. He spat out the glowing stub.

No cigarette.

Sarah was ten minutes late to the spot where she had arranged to meet Michael and Thomas. It was a crossroads in the sheep-tracks, pretty well invisible except to sheep and children. One branch of the track led down the moor to Thomas Wyatt's house.

'Come on, come on,' said Sarah to herself, five minutes later. 'This is typical, typical. Come *on*, I'll freeze to death. Men!'

Sarah was dressed in cords, and yellow boots, and her anorak. Under that were two jerseys, and under her trousers, woolly tights. The wind, when she stood full in it, went through everything like a knife. There was precious little shelter, here.

After three minutes more, she set off down the track towards the Wyatt house. Before she moved she shouted.

'Michael! Thomas! Tommy? Michael?'

Because she guessed it could be some kind of a joke. An ambush. Even with soldiers about, maybe, when real danger might be lurking, Michael would probably have something stupid up his sleeve. As for Thomas — he could be anywhere.

Michael, hiding behind a rock, fingered the open blade of his knife as Sarah approached. For a moment, it was for real. He was a commando, she a spy. He would launch himself upon her, and draw the steel across her throat, from left to right. Bright blood would spurt, and she would die. It was the proper way, the manly way. It was necessary.

As she passed, however, he slowly closed the blade. Sarah had a temper on her, and secretly he was not sure if he could handle her. She was about his size, maybe a

20

little bigger. His father said she was a tomboy, needed taking in hand, which he agreed with, totally. But although it would be more fun to ambush her with an open blade – he did not dare.

With a bloodcurdling roar the intrepid commando launched himself through the air onto the back of his victim. Out of the corner of her eye, Sarah caught the movement. A figure in a combat jacket. Despite herself, she had a burst of fear, but as she fell she recognized the foe. He lay across her, stabbing her furiously with the closed-up knife, and Sarah did not know whether to laugh or spit.

'You're a fool,' she muttered, as she pushed him off. 'One of these days I'll really bash you one.'

Michael, kneeling in the grass, sneered.

'I bet I scared you, though,' he said. 'I could have killed you if I'd wanted to.'

They stood by the fence above Thomas's house as they had so many times before. You did not go down and knock on the door, or walk into the kitchen, as in other people's houses. That was not allowed. They were almost fed up enough to go, to leave him to his fate, by the time he appeared round a corner of the house.

'At ruddy last,' said Michael. And then: 'Oh *no*!'

Thomas was not alone. First his mother, then his father turned the corner. As Thomas raced across the garden, they called him back. His mother was fussing with his anorak, his woolly hat. His father was giving him a lecture.

'My God,' said Michael. 'It's no wonder he's always late for everything. Earache, earache, earache. Don't they ever let up on him?'

Sarah, leaning on the fencepost, shivered slightly in the wind. If you pull that hat down any more, Mrs Wyatt, she thought, you'll pop his head right through.

'Well he is only eight, I suppose,' she said. 'I suppose they worry about him because of that.'

'Nuts,' replied Michael. 'His Dad's a pain, that's all. He never lets him alone. He can't even breathe without permission.'

Thomas was climbing the garden fence.

'Here he comes.'

But no. Thomas had run ten steps only when he was called. His father had a go at him, pointing up towards the ridge, wagging his finger in his face.

'Look at the old devil moaning on. It's ridiculous.'

'There is a war on,' said Sarah. 'Still, I'm glad my Mum and Dad don't carry on like that. They just told me to be careful. But there is a war on.'

'Sarah! Michael!'

Thomas was finally on his way, running up the hill towards them.

'Where we going?' asked Sarah. 'To the den?'

'Let's run,' said Michael. 'Let's leave him.'

'Oh don't be mean.'

'Sarah! Michael! Wait for me.'

Sarah giggled.

'Come on then,' she said. 'Let's give him a run for his money! Teach him to keep *us* waiting!'

By the time Thomas reached the fence they were a hundred yards away, and going strong. He almost tore his jeans getting across the barbed wire.

'Sarah! Come back! Wait!'

They kept on running. He heard Michael shouting something, but the wind whipped it away.

Swine, he thought. But it did not matter much, he'd catch them up. He knew where they'd be going, in weather like this. They'd need somewhere to keep warm.

They'd need some shelter.

Chapter Three

In the sunshine, out of the wind, the soldier had slept. When the sun had left him in shadow, he had awoken. Once more cold, but not so cold. Once more stiff, once more in pain. But he had been able to move, back into the sunshine. Slowly, he had become warmer. His clothes were dry.

The solider stared through the doorway, then around the ruin where he lay. Outside, he could see a long sweep of moorland, green and brown. Occasional cloud shadows raced across the grass, and sheep wandered across the narrow path of his vision. No houses, no fences, nothing. He was very lonely.

Inside the refuge there was also nothing. A few slates that had dropped from the roof when there had been one, some worm-eaten planks, sheep droppings. Not enough small wood, even, to make a fire. He had thought about that for a long time. At night he would need a fire, and the smoke would be invisible. But he did not have the strength, he knew, to gather wood. Maybe later.

There was day-time to consider, also. If the sun went in, or it rained, it would become much colder. But even if he could find small wood, on these desolate, woodless islands, dared he light it? What if someone saw?

Not often, the soldier allowed his mind to wander on his plight. If he did light a fire by day, someone might find him. But who? And if he was *not* found, sometime, sometime soon – what would happen then?

He did not feel hungry, but he had no food. He did not feel as if he was dying, but he could hardly move.

If nobody found him — his comrades, or the islanders, or the British — what then?

The soldier was a young man, he was sixteen years. When these thoughts came to him, he could not dwell on them. He would not. He had no answers.

He had *no* answers.

Sarah allowed Thomas to catch up with them before they reached the den, because she guessed he would soon be crying.

'Come on, Michael,' she panted. 'A joke's a joke. He'll be more trouble than he's worth if we make him bawl.'

Michael slowed down to a jog, then stopped.

'More trouble than he's worth anyway. The best thing about it when the British win is we'll be able to play with proper kids again.'

Sarah did not reply. But she had her thoughts. Sure enough, when Thomas trotted up, his face was on the verge of crumpling.

'You're rotten you two are,' he said. 'I thought you were my friend, Sarah. You're horrible.'

Michael made a noise, then headed off towards the sea.

'Come on,' he said. 'Quit whining, Thomas, you make me sick. Let's get to the den.'

'I'm not coming,' Thomas began. 'It's not fair, I—'

Sarah reached into her anorak pocket and pulled a white paper packet out.

'Stop moaning or you don't get toffee,' she said. 'My Mum made it last night. It's great; real stickjaw.'

Thomas weighed up the position. No point in sulking if it lost you something special. Sarah set off after Michael, and he tagged along.

'Why we going to the sea den, though?' he asked. 'It's much warmer at the other one.'

Michael called back over his shoulder: 'It's more fun. It's got the RT set. We can play at soldiers.'

'Oh gawd,' breathed Sarah. She stopped to wait for Thomas.

'Soldiers,' she said. 'Soldiers, soldiers, soldiers.'

With shaking hands, he cut away the fabric of his trouser leg until the wound was exposed. Fearfully, he touched the blue and purple flesh. Feeling nothing, he probed further, aware of the filthiness of his fingers. The soldier did not even have a handkerchief to use as swab or bandage.

The flesh was moist, with a clear, pinkish fluid weeping from it. He could not understand how it had happened, it was as if a metal claw had grabbed at him. Gingerly, the soldier lifted up a fold of skin. The white bone under it was split and jagged.

He passed out.

The den was fairly sheltered, and the sun was shining brightly on to them. Seabirds screamed as they wheeled above the surf, which crashed and roared constantly. Across the ocean, nothing was visible, except white crests of the breaking rollers. They had all, at Michael's suggestion, scanned the waves for British warships. Nothing.

They were in a circle, their eyes still running from staring at the wind, eating toffee from the paper. Sarah was on a washed-up log, with Thomas near her, on the sand. Michael was seated by his pride and joy, an old ex-Army radio telephone. It did not work, of course. But to him, it was fantastic.

'You're lucky you are, Sarah,' said Thomas. He paused, trying to unstick his teeth. 'I wish my Mum made stuff like this.'

Michael was mocking.

'Your Mum would kill you if she saw you even eating it.' He put on a grown-up voice. 'Thomas Wyatt, how dare you! That rubbish will rot your little toothypegs!'

To get him off Thomas's back, Sarah said: 'She says we need it because we've been invaded. She says toffee's what keeps you going.'

That sounded silly, although her mother *had* said it. Thomas just looked mystified.

'What's she mean by that, though?'

'Oh, I dunno,' said Sarah. 'She was a kid after the last war, right? In England. They had rationing or something. You couldn't get sweets. You couldn't get sugar, even, to make toffee with. So she says we've got to have it now. The principle of the thing.'

Michael smirked.

'She's as daft as you are. Stupid.'

Sarah waved the paper right underneath his nose, on the way to offering it to Thomas.

'You don't have to eat it, Guts. Thomas and me'll be more than happy without your big gob at the trough.'

Michael put on terror.

'No no! Anything but that! Your Mum's fantastic, Sarah.' A stupid, smarmy look. 'Just like you!'

Sarah pretended to throw up.

'Yuk! Here, have some quick. Anything to stick your horrible mouth up. You're revolting.'

After they had been chewing in silence for a while, Thomas asked: 'Did you hear the firing last night? It woke me up.'

Michael was straight into the attack.

'I bet it did. I bet you nearly wet yourself. Did you call out for your Mummy?'

'*I* did,' Sarah said quickly. Let Michael laugh at *her*, if he dared. 'I got in bed with my Mum and Dad. I was petrified.'

26

Michael smiled a big smug smile.

'I didn't hear a thing. I slept like a log. I bet it wasn't that close, anyway.'

'You're wrong then, Cleverdick,' said Thomas triumphantly. 'My Dad says it's very close, and he says it's getting closer all the time. He almost didn't let me come out today, he said it might be dangerous.'

'Yah, dangerous,' went Michael. 'He's wet. *My* old man could hardly wait to get me out of the house. He gets really fed up with me now we can't go to school no more.'

'The poor teacher has to put up with you, though,' said Sarah. 'My Mum reckons it should be a medal job.' She put her finger into her mouth and picked a piece of toffee off a tooth. 'It's funny, though,' she said.

She went back to sucking at the tooth and toffee.

'What?' asked Thomas. 'What's funny?'

'Oh, I dunno,' said Sarah. She waved her arm across the shoreline and the dunes. 'All this lot. I mean, here we are in our den, just as if nothing's happening, and we're at war. Somewhere out there there's ships, and submarines, and planes. And there's soldiers all over everywhere, crawling about with guns. It seems ridiculous.'

Michael laughed.

'You wouldn't think so if you met one face to face. You'd run a mile.'

A withering look from Sarah.

'Fat chance of that though, isn't there? It's other people always get the fun. We're just sitting here, doing nothing, messing about. Fat chance.'

Thomas was wide-eyed.

'You wouldn't *want* to, Sarah? They're despoilers. Evil despoilers.'

'Despoilers,' crowed Michael. 'That's a big word for a little pillock. What does it mean?'

27

Thomas frowned. He did not know he was being mocked.

'Well I . . . well I *think* that's what Dad said. He said they're invaders, and despoilers, and beasts and that. Rapists.'

Sarah and Michael could hardly keep straight faces.

'Rapists! Ooh I say! What do *they* do when they're out then, Tom?'

Thomas realized they were laughing at him. Both of them. He pushed a large chunk of toffee into his mouth so that his jaws were glued. That was that.

Michael said: 'You're daft, you are, Thomas. They're not rapists and despoilers and other stupid names. They're soldiers, that's all. The enemy. And they'll be driven into the sea.'

He pulled his knife from out of his pocket and opened it. He drew the blunt side of the blade across his throat, making a horrible choking noise.

'Or if the gurkhas catch them,' he went on, 'they'll have their throats cut. They've had it, they're all dead men.'

He snapped the knife shut.

'Thomas,' he added. 'They have not got a chance.'

For a while after coming round, the soldier was aware of something different. Something had awoken him, some noise perhaps. He lay listening, tense. The sun had left him once more, in the shadow. He was chilled and faint.

Maybe the wind had died down. Maybe that was it. It did sound less violent. The rushing noise through the old roof timbers and the stonework was quieter.

But that had not been it. There was another noise. He felt fear seeping through him, he felt his body tense, then relax, weakly. He was like a kitten, he had no power. The soldier tried to lift his rifle from the ground beside him, but it would hardly move. He looked at it, willing it to become lighter, to be liftable as it had always been, then tried again.

It was as if it had been bolted to the ground.

Outside the noise came clearly. It was a boot, scraping on a rock. There were men out there, men.

He tried so hard to lift his rifle, or himself, that the sky turned black. Great flashes of red and green light swum through the darkness, the wound in his thigh sent a charge of pain throughout his body like a huge electric shock.

The soldier fell back uselessly, his head hitting the packed earth hard. He bit his bottom lip to stop from screaming, and he tasted blood.

Outside, he heard more feet on stones. Scraping noisily, making no attempt at quietness.

The soldier opened his eyes and stared upwards, the heavens flashing and pulsing as blood drummed through his head.

And the first sheep walked in. It looked at him, as if quite interested, then was followed by its sisters.

The familiar smell was unbearable. The familiar smell from home. He touched a passing sheep, and it stopped, and let him go on touching.

He buried himself in sheep.

Chapter Four

With the toffee finished, they had to decide what to do. Whatever else you thought about school, it was somewhere to be. Looking at the two boys, Sarah realized how much she missed the normal run of things.

Not meaning to, she snapped at Thomas: 'Tommy, why don't you wipe your nose sometimes? There's a big lump of snot hanging out.'

Thomas did not notice the nastiness in her voice. He sniffed, licked, then wiped what was left away with his anorak sleeve.

'What we gonna do?' he asked.

'I know,' said Michael. 'Let's—'

'Play soldiers,' interrupted Sarah, sarkily.

She got a dirty look.

'Wasn't going to say that, Knowall.'

'It's not a bad idea,' said Thomas.

'What *were* you going to say, then?'

'Wouldn't you like to know?'

Sarah stood up and kicked sand. This was stupid, stupid.

'Go on then, Michael,' she said. 'What *were* you going to say?'

He smirked.

'Let's go a treasure hunt,' he said. 'Let's see if we can get some souvenirs.'

'What from?' asked Tommy. 'What souvenirs? What treasure?'

Michael pointed inland.

'Work it out. The battle last night was over there, wasn't it?'

'How do *you* know?' said Sarah. 'You slept through it, remember?'

'Look, if you don't want to hear my idea . . .'

'Shut up, Sarah,' said Thomas. 'Why've you got such a mood on?'

Sarah kicked at the sand harder. The wind caught the grains and made them fly like golden spray. She said nothing.

'So if we walk that way, we might find some wreckage and stuff, right?' Michael's eyes lit up. 'Hey! We might find a plane or something! We might find a blown-up plane!'

Thomas jumped up from the hummock he was sitting on. His face brightened. Then the excitement faded.

'Can't,' he said. 'My Dad and Mum. They told me not to go far. They said I had to stay close. They said Sarah had to look after me.'

'Oh, great,' said Michael.

'Yeah,' said Sarah. 'Absolutely wonderful'.

'Anyway,' said Thomas. 'It could be dangerous, surely? What if we met a gurkha? He'd probably cut our throat.'

'Eat us,' said Sarah, gloomily, not even finding her own jokes funny. 'Drink our blood. Cut our tripes out. Play juggling with our kidneys.'

Michael was disapproving.

'It's not a joke, Sarah,' he said. 'Gurkhas *do* cut people up. It's a fact, that.'

Thomas said nervously: 'Not us, though? I mean, they're on *our* side, ain't they?'

'Not *any*one,' said Sarah. 'It's just a rumour. Propaganda. In war, my Dad said, truth is the first . . . erm. Gets wounded . . . erm. Something, anyway. It's just all lies.'

'Fat lot you know, then,' said Michael. 'Your Dad always talks rubbish, anyway. My Dad says he's . . .'

He stopped. Sarah's face was dangerous.

'What?' she said. 'Your Dad says my Dad's what?'

There was a tense silence.

'Oh shut up quarrelling you two,' said Thomas plaintively. 'It's not much fun anyway without you two going on like cats and dogs. What's it matter about gurkhas killing people anyway? I mean, what about that lot over at Foster's Landing? I mean, if *our* lot kill the enemy, why shouldn't gurkhas, eh?'

Both Sarah and Michael were looking at him, puzzled.

'You what?' asked Sarah. 'What are you talking about?'

'What do you mean, "our lot kill the enemy"?'

Thomas flushed faintly. Maybe he'd got it all wrong. Oh well, what the heck?

'I listened in the night,' he said. 'When I heard the battle. I mean, I couldn't go into their room like Sarah did. It's not allowed. But I heard them talking.'

'What did they say?'

'Well,' said Thomas. He racked his brain. He'd heard snatches, dribs and drabs. And they fitted in with other stuff he'd heard or thought. About that Mr Gregory. And Michael and Sarah were listening.

What the heck?

'He said there were some of them about. My Dad. Young ones. Con . . . cons something.'

'Conscripts, I bet,' said Michael. 'That means they're not in voluntary, they've been forced to fight.'

'*We* know,' said Sarah. 'Don't make a meal of it. Go on, Thomas. What else?'

'Well,' said Thomas. 'He said some of these . . . cons-things . . . had got split off from their army. Over Foster's Landing way. He said the farmers found them, hiding in the straw. The . . . hotheads. I think he said the hotheads.'

Michael nodded, wisely.

'Yeah, that's right,' he said. 'That's where Sid Gregory lives. He drinks, you know.'

I know, thought Thomas. He noted their faces. They were listening intently to him. He liked that; it was nice.

'There's a group of them,' said Sarah. Privately, she knew that Mr Wyatt was one of them, usually. 'Yeah, hotheads sounds about right. So what happened then? To these conscripts?'

Thomas's face went red. He blurted excitedly: 'They . . . my Dad said . . . he said they killed them. Mr Gregory and the other hotheads. He said they banded up. And killed them.'

'*Ace*,' said Michael. 'That's the—'

'No!' said Sarah, harshly. To Thomas's surprise, she was angry. She was glaring at him.

'But—'

'That's a lie, Thomas Wyatt, that's a great big story!'

Michael intervened.

'Oh come on, Sarah,' he said. 'I mean, they *are* the enemy.'

'Oh shut up, you,' snapped Sarah. 'Thomas, that's not true, is it? You made it up.'

It had been so nice to have them listening. He *had* heard something, too. Why *should* Sarah—

'No,' he said. 'I didn't make it up. I . . . I think—'

'Yah, *think*,' spat Sarah, in disgust. 'It's just your normal rubbish. It's just a pack of lies.'

Thomas was going to cry. He knew it. Then Michael started in on him.

'You little weed,' he said. 'You stupid little weed. I don't know why we play with you.'

Thomas pulled his bobble-hat off and crushed it in his hands like a ball. Why were they so foul to him?

He shouted: 'Well it's true, that's all! I'm *not* a liar! I didn't make it up! It's true! I'm going!'

Cramming his hat back on his head, he blundered out of the den and away. Sarah tried to grab him, but she missed.

'Thomas! Tommy! Come back!'

Then she rounded on Michael.

'You rotten pig, Michael. He's only a little boy. You are a rotten pig.'

'Me?' He couldn't believe it. 'Me? Sarah, *you* started it, you know!'

Sarah kicked one more load of sand. It flew in the air, into Michael's face, all over his RT set. When he opened his eyes, she had gone.

Michael cleared the sand from his face and hair with his fingers.

'Women,' he muttered.

With the sheep to comfort him, the soldier soon became happier and stronger. Warmer, as well, because he used them like blankets. He slowly dragged himself into the small stone space and huddled with them.

He wondered if they could tell what he had been, before he put on this uniform of unfamiliar cloth, and carried a rifle instead of his stick. He doubted it. They probably would have huddled with anyone. They were unafraid of man. Uninterested.

But they made him think of home, of the high warm grasses, and the noise, and sunshine. In the pauses as he dragged himself farther inside, he lay resting on the trodden brown earth, smelling sheep and fresh droppings, and aching for his home.

It took a long time, but at last he reached the inner doorway of the ruined hut, and peered through. He had been hoping for a roof, in case of rain. For wood, to build a fire. But there were neither. All it offered that was better, was better shelter from the wind, and more security. The soldier weighed it up.

The inner room was square, like the outer. It had only one door, which he was lying halfway through. So once inside, he could not be taken by surprise.

The soldier remembered the moment he had heard the sheep, had mistaken their scrabbling feet for the boots of men on rock. Even if he fell asleep he would wake before he could be set upon in here. That was good.

Just one thing. Near the centre, was a ring of blackened stones. Someone used it as a fireplace. The soldier let his imagination run. A shepherd, almost certainly. How good that would be, to be found by a shepherd. How good that would be.

Slowly, and with regret, he left the sheep behind. Using his rifle like he would have done his stick, he set off to crawl across the inner room, to reach the wall. Gritting his teeth against the pain.

In the sea den, Michael sat before the RT set, the earphones on his head. He twiddled the dials and listened anxiously.

Nothing.

Almost frantically, he twisted the handle on the side. Where was base? Why would they not come in?

'Patrol calling base. Patrol calling base. Are you receiving me? Over.'

Faintly through the crackling on the phones, he heard something. A flicker of morse, some static whines and whistles, and then – yes! It was a voice!

Michael made a fine adjustment to the dials. The signal was coming in.

'Patrol to base,' he said. 'Patrol to base. Repeat last order. I say repeat last order. Over.'

The message could just be made out. The muscles of his face worked in concentration. Then he relaxed.

'Patrol to base. Patrol to base. I read you loud and clear, loud and clear,' he said. 'Search and destroy affirmative. I repeat, search and destroy affirmative. Roger and out.'

Michael switched off the set, removed the headphones, and hooked them on the side of the casing. He wiped his brow, smiling.

'Roger and out,' he said.

Chapter Five

When Sarah found Thomas, he was sitting on a stone behind a sand dune crying. She did not want to embarrass him, so she waited until he had stopped, more or less. She smiled at the way he pulled his woolly hat off to wipe his face with. She went and sat beside him.

'All right now, Tom? I'll get some more of that toffee for tomorrow. Mum won't give me too much at a time in case my teeth fall out.'

He smiled, wanly.

'Why does he keep getting at me, though, Sarah? I haven't done anything, have I?'

Sarah shrugged. She put her arm round his shoulders and hugged.

'He always gets at me now,' continued Thomas. 'But I'm not a weed, am I? Not any more than I always was.'

Sarah suppressed a laugh, because Thomas was not trying to be funny. He was daft, sometimes. She took her arm away.

'Don't worry, Thomas,' she said. 'He's gone a bit nutty since this lot started, that's all. He loves it. He thinks he's a real soldier, like a grown-up.'

'But he's not though, is he? I mean, he's only just a kid. He's only a few years older than me.'

Sarah made a noise of contempt.

'Of course he's not a real soldier, Dumbo. He just fancies himself. That's why he wears that combat jacket and that silly hat. I mean, a soldier wouldn't wear a bush hat, would he? Not in winter. Daft.'

This had not occurred to Thomas. It amused him. A jungle hat in winter. In *this* place.

'Yeah,' he said. 'That soppy radio, an'all. The way he goes on, you'd think there was someone at the other end, listening. I think he's stupid.'

'Like a savage, my Mum says. All this talk of gurkhas and stuff. He wants to cut some throats, like on the films. She says he needs taking in hand, before the war's the ruin of him. She says it's turned him into a bloodthirsty little devil.'

Thomas said: 'He frightens me sometimes, Sarah. He . . . he reminds me of my Dad.'

Sarah patted him lightly on the bobble-cap, to show she had not noticed this confession. She stood up, and looked at the breakers rolling in.

'At least he tells you things, your Dad,' she said. 'Every time I ask about the war my parents just tell me not to worry. They treat me like a child. Thomas . . .?'

Something in her voice made him glance up, and then away.

'Thomas,' she repeated. 'Look at me. It wasn't true, was it? What you said about those conscripts? Killing them?'

He kept his chin down on his neck, buried. Sarah came across and shoved him down on to his back. She started tickling.

'Thomas! Was it really, *really* true?'

He giggled, desperately, and wriggled. He rolled sideways on the rock, slipping from her grasp. Sarah gave up. She left him, and began to kick a stone.

Thomas, after a few seconds, sat upright. He brushed the sand off his clothes.

'I'm fed up with this war,' he said resentfully. 'It's spoiled everything. Nothing's any fun no more. It's ruinated.'

There was a silence between them. They stood, apart,

in the wind. It tore at their clothes, smelling of sea, and salt, and weed.

Then Michael's voice.

'Hey! You two! I've got this great idea! Come over here!'

He was standing on a low cliff, a hundred yards away. He was waving.

'I've been talking to HQ on radio,' he called. 'I've got this great idea. We're going to hunt a conscript. We're going to find ourselves a soldier, an enemy. We'll search the area, all right?'

Sarah and Thomas did not move, so Michael clambered down towards them.

Nearer, he said: 'It's better than finding souvenirs, you must admit. It's better than finding wreckage. We're going to get ourselves a real live soldier.

'A prisoner of war.'

The soldier had felt sick. With hunger, he supposed. But that had passed. Now he was thirsty, terribly, painfully thirsty.

With trembling fingers, he unscrewed the water-bottle, and placed it to his lips. It was less than half-full, so he filled his mouth slowly, then tilted the bottle upright. It was difficult not to swallow, but he forced himself. He rinsed the water round and round his mouth, until it was thick with spittle, no longer refreshing. Then he swallowed it and tilted the bottle for another mouthful. Before he swallowed this one, he screwed the top back on and laid the bottle down. That was his ration.

The water gone, he moved his shoulders against the lumpy wall, listening for the sheep. But they had gone also. He was quite alone. He felt the inside of his mouth, then his lips, with his tongue. Better. For the moment, he would survive.

Beside him on the earth, on a square of scarf material he had brought from home, the soldier saw his cassette-recorder. It was cheap, and scratchy, and the batteries might be low. Desperately, he wanted to put it to his ears, to press the button, to listen to the tape.

Not yet. The batteries might be low.

Not yet.

Thomas was squawking, and Sarah was furious. Michael, poking at the dead sheep with a stick, was smiling a cocky smile, as if to tell them they were being childish.

'Oh shut up, Thomas Wyatt,' he said. 'You ought to look at that, you know. It'll harden you up for battle.'

Thomas was scrubbing at his hands with a clump of grass. He kept studying them, to see if there was blood or guts on them.

'I almost fell in that,' he said. 'It's disgusting. You had me creeping up on it until I almost put my face right in the blood. I'm going to tell my Mum of you.'

'You are a little weed,' said Michael. 'It's necessary training, this. We've got a job to do. We've got to play our part.'

That was too much for Sarah. She turned on Michael.

'You're sick, you are,' she told him. 'Getting us to crawl along this ditch like that and calling it some stupid "training". I bet you knew that was there all the time, didn't you? I bet you hoped we'd fall right into it. You really are a little savage, Michael.'

'No,' Michael shouted. 'I *didn't* know it was there. And I'm not a savage, I'm a patriot. It's good we've seen this sheep, it's good training for when we catch our prisoner. It's our duty to be ready, there's a *war* on.'

'You're cracked, you are,' said Sarah. 'It's just a dead old sheep.'

Michael pushed his stick right into the heart of the mess.

'Not old, it's *new*, that's the *point*. It's not rotten, Sarah. It's just been hit. It's almost *warm*.'

Thomas and Sarah stared. The sheep, through dull glazed eyes, almost appeared to stare back. And Michael was right. It was not a normal dead sheep. It had not fallen and died, it was not blown with gases, it had not been torn at by night animals. It was smothered with fresh blood, and it had broken bone sticking through its wool. It had been hit.

'By *what*?' hissed Sarah.

'Well, a shell I spose,' said Michael. 'It must've been. It shows how close the battle was. Unless . . . unless it trod on a mine!'

Sarah gave a little scream, and Thomas began to run. Michael, white-faced, grabbed him.

'Stand still! Stand still!'

For half a minute they stood there, exchanging glances. The wind sighed over the moorland, bending the grass and ruffling the dead sheep's wool. Then Sarah said: 'It couldn't've been a mine, could it? Honestly?'

Michael said uncertainly: 'No I . . . I don't think . . . Well.'

Thomas made a small, frightened noise, and Sarah shushed him. She gave a smile, a reassuring smile.

'We'll be all right,' she said. 'We'll get away from here. Just don't move for the moment. Just stand still.'

'Look,' said Michael. 'It can't be a minefield, can it? I mean, there's nothing here to mine. It's just a stray shell, right? It landed in the night and this poor old woolly bought it. It *can't* be a minefield.'

'But what—'

'Look, we've crawled all over, haven't we? We've wandered up and down. If it was a minefield we'd be dead by now. As dead as . . .'

Michael grinned, prodding hard at the sheep.

'Mutton!' he finished.

'You're sick,' said Sarah, faintly.

But Michael had had enough. He gave the corpse a final poke.

'I'm cold,' he said. 'I vote we go to the hut. The one with walls. I want to get out of this wind.'

'But if there *are* mines,' Sarah started.

'Oh *knickers* to the mines!'

Michael jumped away from Sarah and Thomas, who clutched each other, terrified. He did a wild wardance all around them, stamping in every direction.

'There you are, Weedikins,' he panted, when he'd done. 'No mines. Come on, troops. Let's go and get some shelter.'

They began to traverse the moorland in the freezing wind.

Inside the shelter, the lure of the cassette recorder had become too much. The soldier picked it up, and looked at it for a long moment, with love.

He fitted the sponge-padded speakers over his ears gently, and laid the contraption in his lap. He moved his shoulders against the rough stone until he was as comfortable as he could be. He watched the white clouds racing across the blue sky, thinking of his home.

The cassette was already rewound to its starting point. His dirty, stubby finger found the button. And pressed.

As the tape began to hiss, the soldier closed his eyes and rested his head upon the stone behind him.

In three seconds time, those voices. Ah . . . those voices.

'I still think we ought to stalk up to it,' said Michael. 'Just in case.'

'I'm too cold to stalk,' said Thomas. 'Let's just get inside. I wish I'd brought them matches I've got hid. We could have lit the fire again.'

'In case of what, anyway?' Sarah asked Michael. 'You've got stalking on the brain.'

Michael pointed to the shelter with his stick.

'In case we find one, stupid. In case there's a soldier hiding in there.'

Sarah shivered in the wind.

'You're bonkers you are, Michael,' she said. 'What would a soldier be doing here? *Think*, man.'

They were getting very close. Despite Michael's efforts to make them behave like commandos, they were talking loudly. He kept his voice low, to try and get to them.

'They said some got separated off,' he said. 'Thomas's Dad said. Over at Foster's Landing.'

Sarah crowed.

'Oh yes, you've changed *your* tune! Thomas was a little liar then, wasn't he!?'

Remembering Michael's cruelty, Thomas said, to nobody in particular: 'I'm going to tell my Mum of him, anyway.'

'And I suppose you'll do like Mr Gregory's meant to have, will you?' Sarah went on. 'I suppose you'll out with your stupid knife and slit his throat. Nutcase.'

She tossed her head, clearing the windblown hair from her eyes. She gave him a look. Michael, unabashed, hauled his knife out and opened it. He made a gesture in the air.

'If I found one I would,' he said. 'Course I would. They're the enemy. The invaders. That word Thomas said.'

Thomas, not knowing he was being set up, tried to remember it.

'Cons . . .' he began. 'Con—'

'No, you fool,' sneered Michael. 'Rapists!'

'Oh yeah,' said Thomas. 'And despoilers.'

'Oh my God,' said Michael. 'I despair of you.'

He took Thomas by the arm. They were almost at the shelter door. He made a signal to Sarah to stand still.

'Ssh,' he said. 'Shut your mouths the pair of you. We're going in.'

The soldier did not know what made him take the headphones off. By luck or instinct, he pressed the switch to stop, and eased the curved plastic forward over his head. Instantly he heard the other sounds, the outside sounds.

This time there was no mistake. This time it was not sheep. This time it was people.

Surprising himself by his lack of panic, the soldier stuffed the cassette player into his pocket and began to move. Although it cost him much in agony, he began to put himself into position. His position of defence. This time, nothing could catch him unawares.

Michael led the way into the outer building, walking half-crouched, his back to the wall, his knife arm stretched in front of him. Sarah and Thomas followed on, half mockingly, but half joining in the game. They did not giggle, they did not speak.

Slowly, like something from a film, Michael crept up to the door. He gestured to the others to keep well in, then looked through. He stopped, listening and watching.

There was nothing but the wind to hear. And on the shelter floor, nothing new. Planks, stone tiles, rocks, sheep droppings. Except . . . there was a piece of cloth opposite him, a sort of blueish grey in the sunlight. It could be new, it could be old. He could not, truly, remember.

Michael walked confidently through the doorway and waved the others in. Sarah spotted the cloth immediately.

But before she could speak, or move towards it, the soldier, behind them, hardly able to support the weight of his rifle, sick – put pressure on the trigger.

As the rifle jerked and blasted in his hand, he let out a cry of horror.

Which the children did not hear.

Chapter Six

For many moments, the children were deafened by the noise of the shot. They did not hear the soldier's cry, nor did they hear the rock and concrete that clattered to the ground as the bullet struck into the stonework above their heads. They knew the shot had been fired from behind them, and they froze.

Before they turned, at last, Michael and Sarah looked at each other, with wide eyes. Thomas's were closed, screwed tightly, as were his fists. But as the others turned, so did he. As he opened his eyes, he began to make a sound.

It was a high, whining noise, a jerky squeaking, and it was quite nerve-racking. Sarah and Michael, wound up like wire strings, could hardly bear it, it was so unhuman. Whatever little courage they had left was being drained by it.

The soldier was still covering them with his rifle; they were under guard. But both of them could see that he was ill. He was propped crookedly against the wall, beside the doorway, almost as if he were broken in the middle, as if at any moment he might fold up like a deckchair, and collapse. His face, behind a growth of stubble, was grey and yellowish-white, twisted with pain. The eyes were not full-open.

And he was young. Despite the greyness of his skin, despite the stubble, despite the gun, he was young. Sarah, for some reason, was deeply shocked by this. He was not much older than she was, or Michael. A matter of a few years. He was a *boy*.

Almost as if he was responding to Thomas's awful

whine, the soldier moved his gun. It wavered, wandered even farther away from them. He was staring, staring, staring. The rifle shook.

It was too much for Michael. He hissed at Thomas, violently: 'Shut it, Thomas! For God's sake stop that row.'

At Michael's voice, the rifle twitched up towards them, as if jerked. Thomas sprang at Sarah, and hid his face in her anorak. She stiffly put her arm round him.

'There there,' she said. 'There there. Don't shoot, please; don't shoot. Please don't shoot.'

Thomas, unable to bear the thought of dying with his eyes hidden, pulled his head clear.

'He's going to kill us,' he said. His voice began to rise. 'He's going to shoot us!'

'Shut it,' snapped Michael. 'Thomas! Shut it!'

The rifle wavered, but Thomas was still. Sarah said carefully: 'Please don't shoot us, Mister. We're only harmless children. Please.'

The eyes of the soldier, not fully open, moved and settled on her face. They seemed brown, and drenched in agony. They moved away, and Sarah followed their direction. She understood.

'Michael,' she whispered. 'God, you *fool*. Michael!'

She gestured, still with care. Michael saw the knife, in his own hand, as if it were in someone else's. As if it were a bomb. He was standing in a commando stance, threatening. He swallowed.

'It's a toy,' Sarah told the soldier. 'Do you understand? It's a toy.'

Humbly, Michael allowed her to take the knife. She closed it carefully, without a click, and gave it back to him. Michael slipped it into his pocket, and stood upright. Not like a commando, anything but that. Like a child. The rifle barrel, as if in response, wavered slowly downwards, towards the earth.

'I want my Mum,' said Thomas, low and whiny. 'Sarah, make him let us go. *Make* him.'

Michael whispered: 'I'm going to make a dash! I'm going to—'

'No!'

The rifle twitched once more. Sarah, the muscles in her face aching, smiled.

'We don't want to hurt you, sir,' she said, slowly. 'We're just kids playing. We don't want to hurt you. Do . . . you . . . understand?'

Perhaps the soldier tried to smile. His face changed, then he groaned. The rifle barrel drooped until it almost touched the ground.

'Not hurt,' he said. It was a croak, hardly audible. 'Am cold. Am food.'

He said something else, in a language they did not know. His eyes closed, and the muzzle rested on the soil.

Michael, staring at him fascinated, whispered to Sarah: 'He's useless! We could rush him! We could get that gun and kill him! I—'

He broke off as the brown eyes opened. Sarah whispered: 'Shut up, Michael. You'll get *us* killed. *Please* shut up.'

The soldier blinked. He spoke to them in his own language, saw their blank faces.

'Am hungry,' he finished up.

Sarah, waiting for a polite moment or two, said: 'Can we go, sir? Please. We'd better go now, honestly. Will you let us go?'

After a moment, the soldier moved his soldiers. His face tensed in pain. His eyes closed, then opened.

'No tell soldier,' he whispered. 'Please. Am hurt. No tell soldier.'

Thomas Wyatt suddenly jumped away sideways from Sarah and shouted.

'My Dad'll do you in, mate! You dirty rapist! My Dad'll bring his—'

Impossible to tell which of the three of them was more shocked. The soldier waved his gun, wildly. Sarah became rooted to the ground – and Michael sprang. He seized Thomas by the shoulder and clamped his other hand over his mouth.

'Shut up!' he shouted. Then there was only the wind, and Michael's panting. Slowly the soldier lowered the gun to the earth. He could hardly keep his eyes upon them.

'Friend,' he said. It was almost a breath, only. 'Am friend.'

After fifteen seconds, Sarah took Thomas by the arm. She started to guide him past the soldier.

'Out,' she said softly. 'Go on, Tom, get out. Slowly. Slowly. Out.'

When they were almost in the inner doorway, the soldier opened his eyes. All three of them turned to stone.

His face changed. Maybe he tried to smile. They could barely hear his voice.

'Am friend. Please. No tell the soldier.'

They watched him intently until his eyes drooped closed. Then they left. By the time they reached the outer doorway, they were running as if the devil himself were after them . . .

Thomas left the shelter first, and Thomas left it like a bat out of hell. They were almost halfway down the moor, and he was well in front, before Michael realized which direction he was taking.

He shouted to Sarah: 'He's going home! The little halfwit's going home! Stop him, Sarah! He'll tell his Mum and Dad!'

Sarah was between Michael and Thomas, and she put on a spurt. The experience in the shelter was too close in the past, and she was running too hard, to think clearly, but on that score there was no question. Thomas's parents must not know.

She was pretty close to Thomas, who was running like an Olympic madman, when Michael overtook her. He was bouncing from hummock to hummock, grunting as he bounced. It was another hundred yards before he caught him, though, because Thomas had seen him from the corner of his eye. He had dodged and weaved and wailed.

'I want my Mum,' he screeched. 'Leave me alone! I want my Mum!'

Michael knocked him over with a rugby tackle, and when Sarah panted up, they were still rolling together on the ground, with Thomas feebly punching at Michael's face and chest.

'I want my Mum,' he was screaming. 'You bloody pig, let me go! I want my Mum!'

Sarah dropped beside them, on her knees.

'Thomas,' she gasped, between breaths. 'Thomas! Don't be daft. Don't be crazy.'

Thomas pulled away from Michael and rolled into a hummock, hunched up. He hid his face in the grass, having a tantrum.

Sarah said. 'You're safe, Thomas, you're safe. You don't *need* your Mummy.'

Michael turned onto his back and lay staring at the cold blue sky, panting.

'You're a pain you are, Tommy,' he said. 'A pain in the bum. You'll ruin everything. Keep your rotten mouth shut.'

'Oh leave him be,' said Sarah. She tried to touch Thomas, but he wriggled and spat like a wild animal. She moved away, half-smiling.

'It was a terrible shock,' she went on. 'I almost died of fright. Leave him be for a minute. He'll recover.'

In the shelter, the soldier did not move for a very long time. He listened to the children run away, and his stomach was hollow with fear. They would go home, naturally they would go home. They would tell their parents what they had seen, what they had found, and their parents . . . what?

The soldier tried to lift his rifle, as a gesture of self-defence. He saw soldiers coming for him, their guns ready. But his rifle, as before, seemed bolted to the ground, this time by its muzzle. He let it drop beside him, and with one weak hand slipped on the safety catch. No more shooting.

A sweat broke out on his brow. How terrible, that he had shot at children. How terrible. He raised his eyes to the wall, where a scar of clean stone showed where his shot had struck. He could not even raise a hand to wipe the sweat that chilled quickly on his face.

After many minutes, the soldier had decided that he must move, must find more shelter, shelter somewhere else. After many minutes more, he knew it was impossible. Here he must stay, to see what was in store for him. Here he must stay.

He looked across at the blue-grey material he had left behind him when he moved, the scarf which the boy who played at soldiers had not seen, or had not been warned by. He almost smiled. Poor boy. A real soldier would not have made that mistake.

The smile died. A real soldier, perhaps, would have killed those children, to avoid detection. Truly, it had been the only way.

After a few minutes more, he set himself this objective: one thing and one thing only he would do, he must. He would reach that scarf, and hide it in his pocket. Never more would it give him away. Then later, if he had the strength, he would move back to this position. And if soldiers came, he could . . .

Who knew?

Down at the sea den, Sarah was watching Michael's face with ever more amazement. In his turn, he would not meet her eye. Thomas, who'd got bored with their discussion after they'd convinced him – or forced him to agree – about the need for secrecy, was trying to hit sea birds with stones. But he was listening, all the same.

'All right then, Michael,' Sarah said, her voice tight and edgy. 'If you've got a plan, tell me it. Why won't you *tell* me it?'

Michael's voice was too quiet for Thomas to catch, so he dropped his hand to his side and turned to them.

Sarah had not heard, either. Or could not believe it. She was pale.

'Did I hear you right, Michael?' she said. 'Would you repeat that, please?'

Thomas glanced from face to face. It was good, this. Michael looked at Sarah, defiantly. He looked at her and spoke. His voice was clear and loud.

'Yes,' he said. 'I will repeat it. I said we've got to kill him, Sarah.'

Thomas dropped his stone.

'We've got to kill the soldier.'

Chapter Seven

For a moment, Thomas was horrified. Then he was delighted. Sarah was going to blow her top. Now they'd have some fun! He secretly thought that she could batter Michael, if she put her mind to it. It would be a smashing fight.

Then, to his disappointment, Sarah's expression changed. She said, quietly, to Michael: 'You're joking, aren't you, Michael? You *are* trying to pull my leg?'

Michael faced up to her. It was like a school discussion, Thomas thought. When they were going through a project. He'd much rather have seen a fight.

'No, Sarah,' Michael replied. 'I'm serious.'

'You're disgusting, then,' said Sarah. 'You want to see a doctor, you do. You're sick.'

She turned away. Michael grinned at Thomas. He made a 'screwy' sign with his finger at his temple, and pointed at her back. Thomas nodded vigorously.

'Look,' said Michael, in a voice of sweet reason. 'Look, Sarah, either way he dies, doesn't he? If we leave him, he dies of cold and starves. How long does a sheep last, even, if it gets sick up there? He hasn't got a fur coat, Sarah, he's a *man*.'

Sarah rounded on him furiously.

'Yes,' she shouted. 'He's a man! He's a human being! And what are you saying — we've got to kill him! You're crazy, Michael. You're disgusting.'

He waited for the flash of anger to pass. He kept his cool. He chose his time.

'Look,' he went on. 'Yes, all that's true. But answer me. What's the choices? I'm right, aren't I? If we leave him, he dies of cold or starves. Doesn't he, Sarah? Doesn't he? How long do *you* think he'd last out?'

She did not answer. Michael smiled at Thomas, and put his finger to his lips: don't you say anything, he signalled.

'All right,' said Michael. 'If we leave him he dies. And if we tell on him – what then? The hotheads get him, that's what. That Mr Gregory and his gang. Even Thomas's Dad maybe – how would he go on if he knew he'd fired at his little son?'

Cripes, thought Thomas. Hey, that's right! His Dad wouldn't stand for anything like that. He'd be furious! He was about to say so, but Sarah got in first.

'What do you mean, "fired at"?' she demanded. She turned and faced Michael, her face red. 'You know damn well he didn't mean to kill us, Michael. His gun went off, that's all. He's sick. He's wounded.'

Thomas burst out: 'You're stupid, Sarah! Of course he tried to kill us! It's his job!'

Michael smiled.

'Well even if he didn't,' he said, 'it's only luck we lived to tell the tale, isn't it? And it would still have been murder, wouldn't it? If the bullet had killed Tommy, say?'

Sarah was confused.

'But he's a wounded man,' she said. 'He looked terrible. I think he must have been shot or something.'

'If he was shot it was our side what did it, though,' said Thomas. He was excited by his cleverness. 'Because he was shooting *them*. He's the enemy. He murders British soldiers.'

'Exactly,' said Michael. 'If you think about it, Sarah, he's out to kill the lot of us in the end. He's here to ruin and destroy.'

'Yeah,' said Thomas, eagerly. 'He's a rapist and desp—'

'Shut up Thomas, yeah,' said Michael. 'They've ruined everything, and we didn't *ask* them in, did we? They've invaded us and mucked the place up. They've smashed the radios, and the phones, and they've stole stuff and killed sheep and messed up lots of houses. And there's mines all over, and the beaches are ruined, and the lot. They've wrecked the place.'

'My Dad says it's wrecked for good,' said Thomas. 'Even when the Brits have seen them off. Even when the gurkhas have slit their throats and chucked them in the sea. It'll be years before it's safe again. The mines are everywhere. They've ruinated everything.'

Sarah's parents would agree with that, she knew. They reckoned it was even worse. Whoever won the war, if the place was turned into some kind of fort, or garrison, it was finished. There'd be soldiers and sailors everywhere, drunk and bored, fighting and smashing and stealing. And there'd be workers brought in to build roads and airports, and the place would be like a seaport or a Wild West town. It would be violent and full of crime.

Seeing her deep in thought, Michael continued the attack. He did it craftily, he did not rant. He kept his reasonable, I've-thought-it-through approach.

'Thomas is right, see,' he said. 'There's no denying it. He might be a human being, like you said, but he's still a murderer; he's got to be, it's his job. He could've killed dozens of soldiers for all we know, couldn't he? If he's been hit, it's his own fault in a way. He shouldn't *be* here, should he?'

'But to kill him, Michael. That's appalling.'

Thomas said: 'He'll die anyw—'

'Shut up, Thomas. Look, Sarah, it'll help him, in a way. A quick, clean . . . look, anyway, it's our duty. It's our patriotic duty, to do our bit, to show the grown-ups that we care.'

Sarah did not answer. She was looking at the sand beneath her feet.

'We've got to swear,' said Michael. 'We've got to form a solemn ring and swear.'

She glanced up, as if to argue.

'And if you don't swear,' he said. 'You're not a patriot. You're a traitor.'

It had taken the soldier half an hour to reach his scarf, but now he had it. He lay face downwards on the earth, holding it to his mouth and nose. It was a present from his family, and faintly, very faintly, it still smelled of home.

After a few minutes, he transferred it to the side pocket of his combat coat where he kept his other precious item, the cassette player, and he let his fingers feel that, gently, for a while. Earlier, some days ago, he had had another treasure, a pocket diary that he wrote his thoughts in, to show his brother and sisters when he returned home. But he had lost that, or someone had stolen it, maybe, to make cigarette papers from the leaves.

His sickness and exhaustion came and went in long waves. At the moment, the soldier did not feel unwell, was not in much great pain, but was very heavy. There was high sun on his back, and he was warm and sleepy. He knew he should get back, take up his best position of defence. He yawned. He listened to the wind.

He slept.

Sarah finally agreed to swear because she could see no other way. Some of the things Michael said revolted her, others she did not believe, and she also knew he was deliberately not considering some of the possibilities.

But if she did not swear, one thing was bound to

happen. Michael and Thomas would tell their parents, if only to spite her. Sarah could not imagine what would happen then, but the prospect frightened her. Whether or not the Foster's Landing tale was true, she did not trust Mr Wyatt an inch. She had often heard her parents talk about him, and sometimes she had been allowed to join in. Mr Wyatt was capable of anything.

Before she agreed to swear, Sarah insisted on some conditions, that would buy time. Although she did not fully know how, she could sense that time was vital. Nothing must be allowed to happen in a rush.

'All right,' she lied to Michael. 'You've convinced me. But before we do it, we've got to get some food and drink for him, and make him comfortable.'

'But that's daft,' said Thomas, disappointed. 'Why waste time? Let's do our patriotic duty now.'

It had occurred to him that patriotic duty was a good excuse. If there was any trouble over this, even *his* Dad couldn't get het up if he'd been doing patriotic duty. He was a patriot himself, was Dad, a proper one. It meant a lot to him. The sooner they could do it, the sooner he'd feel safe.

Michael was not taken in by Sarah, but he was happy enough she'd agreed to swear. If she had any secret plans, he could still outwit her. And if she was hoping he'd just get fed up of it, she had another think coming. He could handle her delaying tactics.

'You're nuts, you are,' he said, just for the sake of it. 'That's not logical.'

'Never you mind,' replied Sarah, calmly. 'Either we get him some food and stuff and a blanket, or I'm not swearing. Take it or leave it.'

To stop them arguing, Thomas said: 'I've got them matches in my room. I nicked them three weeks ago. We could light a fire, warm him up.'

'Good idea,' said Sarah. 'Warm us up, an'all. This wind's bitter.'

'Suit yourselves, then,' said Michael. 'I think you're both a pair of weeds, but suit yourselves. Now – how are we going to swear?' He pulled his knife out. 'Shall we cut our fingers? Do a blood swear?'

A look of panic crossed Thomas's face.

'Do we have to? I might be sick.'

Sarah laughed. Great little murderer he was going to be. She did not say so, though.

'Hands in the middle, fingers touching,' she said. 'We'll have all the blood we'll ever need later. *Right*, Michael?'

He made a face at her.

'Right,' he said.

They walked three times round in one direction, three times in the other.

'I swear,' said Michael. 'To kill the soldier.'

They walked three times back, then round once more.

'I swear,' said Thomas. 'To kill the soldier.'

They walked three times one way, reversed, and three times back again.

'I swear,' said Sarah.

She stopped. The others did not speak. Their fingers were all still touching.

'To kill the soldier,' Sarah said.

She pulled her hand away, slapping it noisily against her thigh.

'I'm going home to get the stuff,' she said. 'I'll get food and tea and a kettle and stuff. And some blankets.'

'What's up, Sarah?' Michael asked, sarcastically. 'Don't you trust us to get anything?'

'Yes,' said Sarah. 'I trust Thomas to get some matches and some paper, to start the fire with. You, no, I don't trust you. You just wait, I won't be long.'

'Halfway down the moor where the shelter is we'll meet,' said Michael. 'And for God's sake don't let him see you, right? Apart from anything else, you might get shot.'

'Teach your auntie to milk cows,' said Sarah. She pushed between them and climbed rapidly over a dune. She disappeared.

As she set off for home, away from the sand and sea, she heard Michael shouting after her.

'You can't go back on a swear, remember! You can't go back on a swear.'

Then she was alone.

Chapter Eight

The soldier rose through the depths of sleep fast and terrified. He had been dreaming; frightening, fractured dreams, about war and death. But suddenly, the dream changed. It became real.

He surfaced, and awoke, fully aware of what he had done. He had left his rifle propped against the wall. When he had crawled to get the scarf – he had left his rifle.

The soldier lay on the ground, and lifted his head. Waves of nausea swept through him, followed by a raw pain from his wounded leg. He was in a trough, he was fevered, appallingly ill. The sleep, far from making him fitter, had brought in the next wave of pain and discomfort.

Through blurred eyes, he saw the rifle, resting against the wall by the doorway. Not three metres distant, but a lifetime. How could he have forgotten it, how?

Dimly, he remembered. He had used it to lever himself to his knees when he had made his attempt for the scarf. He had pushed it to the wall, then lifted it, step by step, resting the barrel on a higher stone each time, until it formed a bar he could pull himself up on. When he had set off to crawl across the shelter – he had forgotten it.

Now, it would be impossible to reach until the next wave came, the wave of comparative well-being. But he knew he could not wait. He could not lie here, in full view if anyone came through the outer door, and without a weapon. That was insane.

So he breathed deeply. For two minutes, three, five. He pulled in air slowly until his lungs were full, then gently expended it. From time to time the rhythm broke, he panted nauseously. But gradually his eyes began to clear.

Gritting his teeth against the pain, the soldier moved one leg, then the other. Sweat broke out on his forehead, but he moved. He closed his eyes and prayed for many seconds, and then he moved again. He moved.

Michael was on his RT set. Thomas stood at a respectful distance – officer and man – and listened. He wished he could have a go sometimes, but Michael never let him. Maybe after they'd done all this together . . .

'Patrol to base, patrol to base,' said Michael. 'I read you loud and clear. I will stand guard over the enemy. I will stand guard. Roger and out.'

He clicked the switch to 'off' and turned to Thomas. He pulled the headphones off.

'Hey, it's great this, isn't it?' he said. 'It's not a game any more. It's real. Absolutely ace.'

Thomas nodded enthusiastically. Then he voiced the little doubt he had.

'Do . . . do you think she'll do it, though? Do you think she'll go through with it?'

'She promised, didn't she?' said Michael. 'She swore like the rest of us? Death to the enemy! Fantastic!'

He clenched his fist into a glorious salute. It irritated him to see that Thomas still was not convinced. He'd not have thought that he was bright enough.

'Only when you gave in about the food, though,' said Thomas. 'That seems daft to me, to get him food and drink and blankets. Then to kill him. It's potty.'

Michael gave a laugh that he hoped sounded like his father's.

'Female logic, Thomas. There's no rhyme or reason to it. But it does no harm to humour them, I always say. Don't worry your head about it.'

'Mm,' went Thomas. Then: 'I could see her point in a way, though. I mean, him with the gun and that. And us with nothing. It might lull him into a sense of false . . . thingy. Mightn't it?'

'A sense of false security,' said Michael. 'Yeah, course it might. He might even go off to kip if he's got some food in him, who knows? That'd make life easier.' He grinned. 'For us!'

Thomas swallowed. Michael still looked happy, and relaxed, as if nothing was about to happen. The butterflies in his own stomach were turning cartwheels.

He said quietly: 'She didn't give you a lot of choice, in the end, did she? It was either you give in – or no swearing.'

Michael was getting the drift. He could smell blue funk. He told Thomas airily: 'Don't kid yourself. I'd've talked her round. I was dead crafty, you know. Like all that crap about him being a human being and so on. He's just a bloody murderer, but I didn't say so, did I? It serves him right if he's been shot. It serves him right to suffer, he ought to die in rotten agony, he's a prisoner of war. But I didn't say so, did I? I didn't frighten Auntie Sarah off.'

Thomas shook his head. He shivered, and pulled his hat down further over his ears. A cloud covered the sun. It was freezing. Michael took him by the arm, not gently.

'Look,' he said. 'You think that too, don't you? You think he deserves to suffer? You're not a dirty traitor, are you, Thomas Wyatt?'

Thomas jerked his arm away.

'Nah,' he said. 'Course I'm not. I'm just cold, that's all.'

'Good. Cause if you *are* . . .'

Michael left the rest unsaid. They both moved into a sheltered spot behind the dune while the sun was behind the cloud. The seabirds screamed.

'Michael?'

'Yeah?'

'How you . . .? How we . . .? What exactly are we going to do? To . . . you know? Kill him. How *do* you kill a man?'

Michael sat down on a hummock.

'Well,' he said. 'There's lots of ways, aren't there? I mean, it would be easier if he didn't have the gun, granted. Maybe we can let you sneak up on him, and snatch the thing away!'

'What?!' squeaked Thomas. 'Me! Sneak up on him?'

Michael laughed.

'I'm pulling your leg, you twit. I wouldn't trust you to take a dummy off a baby. Relax.'

Relax, thought Thomas. Fat chance. He said sulkily: 'What if he sees us coming, though? What if he shoots us?'

'He won't,' said Michael. 'That's why I agreed to let Nellie Knickerleg get the food and stuff. We'll lull him. Make him sleepy. I might even get my Mum's sleeping pills or something. Put some in his drink to make sure. Or even some poison from the barn. That'd be another way.'

'But what if they caught you at it?'

'Yeah,' replied Michael. 'They might.' He reached into his pocket and the knife appeared. He opened the blade and pretended to tickle Thomas's nose with it. Thomas drew back. 'They might, and that's the problem. But I don't really think it's necessary at all. There are other ways. A commando knife, for instance.'

Thomas swallowed.

'Could you knife him honestly?' he asked. 'Groo, I'd throw up. I'd puke.'

Michael said: 'I'd stick it in his neck and pull. I'd slice it through his jugular and watch the blood squirt. I could do it.'

Thomas licked dry lips.

'Hell, Michael. That's horrible.'

Michael snapped the knife shut.

'It's not a commando knife, though, is it? It's not big enough. No, it'll be a battering job, I reckon. We'll have to batter him.'

'What? With a hammer or something? Will you nick one off your Dad?'

Michael took Thomas by the wrist and squeezed.

'We, Thomas, not just me. No, we don't need a hammer, do we? All we've got to do is give him food and keep him occupied. While he's noshing, we get behind him with a rock, right? The biggest rock we can lift.'

Easing his fingers from Thomas's wrist, he bent over and lifted a rock. He held it at waist height. When he let it go, it hit the sand with an ugly thud. Again, Thomas's mouth went dry. It seemed a pity, now, that this had happened. It didn't seem as if killing this bloke was actually going to be much fun. It seemed a pity he'd had to swear.

'And there you are,' said Michael. 'We drop it on his bonce. Crunch. A deado. A corpse. Simple.' He smiled unpleasantly. 'What d'you think?'

Thomas's voice was just above a whisper.

'It . . . sounds all right,' he said. 'We'd . . . we'd better stand well clear though. There could be lots of blood.' An idea came to him; a good idea, he thought. 'Wouldn't it . . . it would be easier, in a way, to let the grown-ups do it, wouldn't it?'

'Chicken,' mocked Michael.

'No I'm not. No. But . . . it'll be hell's messy, Michael. We'd better stand well clear.'

Michael gave him another nasty smile.

'Well you can't duck out, you know. So you'd better run along, hadn't you? And get those matches that you're always on about, and some paper. To light a fire. He's going to be comfortable when he dies, this one. *Dead* comfortable.'

The soldier was more than halfway to the rifle, but he knew he could not make it. He had lain still for five minutes waiting for the pain to go away, but it would not go. He blinked as rapidly as he could bear, to clear his eyes, but they would not clear. He could hardly lift his head to look at the rifle, and he could not focus on it.

For the moment, he gave up. He allowed the waves of pain and nausea to engulf his senses. He drifted away. The image of the rifle shimmered in his eyes as he became unconscious.

Michael approached the shelter with extraordinary caution. Near the bottom of the moor he watched and waited for minutes until he was certain there was no sign of movement, then he crawled from rock to hummock on a route which kept him well out of the line of vision from the doorway. When he reached the stone walls, he hardly breathed, his face buried in the grass to deaden any sound, until he had his lungs properly under control.

He considered the idea of climbing up and looking over, into the shelter from above. But he rejected that. If a stone should fall, or he should slip, it would mean disaster. But by the time he had crept round to the doorway, his heart was thumping madly and he was sweating.

Then he was there. Through a crack in the stonework, and then through the door itself, he could see that the outer part was empty. Michael ducked into it, and began the long creep round the inside wall to the next hazard. As he got nearer and nearer the point of maximum danger, he became oddly confident. The place was too silent for danger, he was sure. Something had happened. Something to his advantage.

He put his head round gingerly, and saw immediately that he was right. The soldier was sprawled face downwards, one leg stretched out, the other bent as if to push himself along. His head rested on one bent arm; the other was outstretched. Michael was much more observant this time. The soldier did not have his gun.

Michael stood upright and walked quietly into the inner shelter. The rifle was soon beside his hand, and he picked it up. He went up to the soldier, to see if he was dead. No. He was breathing, quite noisily, the breaths not regular. Michael could see his face: grey, sicker than before. He was suddenly afraid that the soldier might die. Before he could shoot him.

Biting his lip, he searched for the safety catch, thanking his stars that he knew about guns. The safety catch was easy to locate, and it was on. Michael pushed it to off. He seized the short bolt and cocked the gun, trying to do it quietly at first, then giving up. That was impossible.

As he jerked it back, wincing at the terrific noise it seemed to make, he watched the soldier. Yes, he stirred. Michael watched and waited. He could smell his sweat. The soldier became still.

Very slowly, Micahel raised the rifle to his shoulder. He squinted down the barrel. The soldier's face was in front of him. Bone of skull, brown, dirty, stubble-covered cheek. Closed eyes, the eyelids trembling.

Michael pulled his finger until the first pressure of the trigger was taken up. One squeeze now. Just one squeeze.

'I'll kill you,' he whispered. 'You're the *enemy*.'

Chapter Nine

The nearer Thomas got to home, the more nervous he became. What if his Dad was home? What if his Mum saw him? What if, what if, what if?

He stood at the wire fence for some time, looking at the lonely little house. There was smoke coming from the chimney, naturally. But there was no other sign of life. No Land Rover, either. Perhaps Mum had gone out to help with the sheep? Perhaps pigs could fly . . .

Thomas gulped, and swung his leg over the fence. He kept to the side of the field, so that his mother could not see him from the kitchen window. What would he *say* if she found him? As he ducked in through the side door, he actually closed his eyes for a moment. He was halfway up the stairs before he dared to breathe.

A stair creaked, and Thomas turned to ice. But he could hear the radio in the kitchen, with unusual, sort of military music coming from it. She could not hear above it, obviously. But he still trod carefully. Only two more creaks before he reached the top . . .

Sarah came downstairs with a blanket over her arm, a picnic kettle, and a plastic bottle for water. She would have to smuggle the kettle outside, though – she was not allowed cooking-fires on the moors – and she decided it would be a good idea to keep the blanket out of sight, as well. Milk and sandwiches were no problem. In fact, she had asked her mother for some before she'd gone upstairs.

She unlatched the kitchen door and went in.

'Hello, love,' said Mum. 'Ready to go are you? I'm just finishing the sandwiches.'

There were plenty of them, because her mother was like that: she did not mind at all making sandwiches for three. Beside them on the kitchen table was a blue and white china jug of milk.

'Thanks, Mum,' said Sarah. 'We thought it'd be good fun, you know. A picnic by the sea.'

'You will be careful, won't you? Your Dad says there might be Army about, mopping up or whatever they call it. It was a big do last night, lots of casualties apparently.' She waggled her eyebrows mock-fiercely. 'Who knows, you might run into that man Gregory and his gang!'

They both smiled, then her mother added: 'Joking aside, though, you haven't seen anything, have you? Any sign of all that fuss? I know it seems daft with all that empty moorland, but I am a *bit* worried. There could be danger out there.'

Sarah shook her head.

'No, not a thing, Mum. And of course we'll be careful. Even Thomas is with us, so it can't be that bad, can it? You know what his Dad's like.'

Her mother nodded.

'Not just his Dad, either,' she agreed. 'I expect a picnic will be a real treat for him, poor little devil.'

It crossed Sarah's mind to tell her mother, then, just to come out with the truth. She would know what to do. She would know how to help the soldier. The words hovered on her lips. It would have been nice. It would have got it off her chest, made someone else responsible.

But she did not tell. If she did, and something went wrong . . . If her mother felt, because Thomas was involved, that his parents must be warned . . . No. For the moment, the secret must be kept. It was safer that way. Even for the soldier . . .

Two minutes later, Sarah left the house. When her mother was back in the kitchen, she filled the bottle at the standpipe, screwed the top down hard, and gathered up the blanket. The jug was difficult. She might spill a drop or two.

But she would manage.

Thomas, creeping about his bedroom with an armful of comics, was getting deeper and deeper into panic. He had never realized before just how much his floorboards creaked, just how easy it was to hear things from one part of their house to another.

Downstairs, he could hear his mother clattering about, and even over the wireless – turned down very low, and still churning out the strange music – he could hear her muttering from time to time. She talked a lot to herself, his Mum did – there was no one else to speak to most of the time, she said – and he liked it. But today, it was getting on his nerves.

Moving over to his chest of drawers, Thomas started to pull the bottom drawer out, without putting down the comics. Standing there, he began to root through socks and underpants with his free hand.

Funny. The matches were not there. But he was positive that was the drawer, positive. Thomas was trembling. At each new noise downstairs he became more tense. It was the bottom drawer. *Positive.*

Ah! No, he'd – Thomas pushed the drawer in and jerked the top drawer out. Halfway, it stuck. He paused, almost whimpering. The noise he must be making! She'd hear. She'd *have* to hear. Gritting his teeth, and still holding the bundle of comics in his other hand, he tried jerking the drawer, that way and this. Come *out,* he whispered. Come *out!*

70

It did. On a sideways, backwards jerk, the drawer flew free. It slipped out all the way, and fell to the floor with a bang. Thomas still had hold of it, but he was not strong enough to keep it off the ground.

Amid the shirts and school shorts were the matches. The box was half open and they were everywhere.

Thomas waited, petrified. His mouth was open, his heart was fluttering in his chest. After what seemed like an incredible pause, he heard the kitchen door pulled open. Another pause.

'Thomas?' His mother's voice was puzzled. 'Is that you, Thomas? What's going on?'

As he heard her footsteps on the stairs, Thomas, hopelessly, tried to cover up the matches. Every time he picked a few up, though, the others spread wider. As the door handle rattled he pushed the comics in among the clothes, hoping that they would hide them.

'Thomas?' Thomas Wyatt closed his eyes. 'Thomas, what *are* you up to, you bad boy? Why are you at home? Thomas, just *look* at this mess!'

Thomas looked.

'I was . . . I was . . .'

His mother's voice changed.

'What's that in your hand? Are those *matches*? You *bad* boy, Thomas. You wicked, wicked boy!'

On the pillow of his bed, Thomas spotted Red Bear. Oh, help me now, he thought.

Sarah had been leaning on the fence above the Wyatt house for fifteen minutes before she began to worry that he might not come. He could never be relied on to be on time, because you never knew what might happen if he met one or other of his parents. But he usually made it in the end.

She checked her watch for the umpteenth time.

'Come *on*, Thomas,' she said, half aloud. 'Let's be *having* you. Oh, the useless, useless boy.'

Sarah shifted the blanket higher over her shoulder. She thought about what her mother had said, and panic fluttered in her stomach.

Oh come *on*, Thomas. You must *hurry*.

Thomas was lying with Red Bear now, and he had stopped crying. As he sniffled though, he was still determined. He would run away from home. When this rotten war was over, he was going to pack his schoolbag with bread and stuff, and a bottle of lemonade, and he would run away from home. He wondered how difficult it was to stow away.

Thomas's resentment at being found out gave way slowly to a resentment that he would be missing all the fun. Even now, he guessed, Sarah and Michael would be feeding up the soldier, and watching him as he settled down to sleep. Then – the death.

He sat up angrily and flung Red Bear to the floor.

It wasn't *fair*. Why should they do all the good things and he be stuck in his room until his Dad came home? *That* might be ages, in any case. And his Mum had said he must not move till then. Under any circumstances.

Another, worse, thought flew into Thomas's mind. If he did not kill the soldier, he would not have been a patriot. And all the bad things would be ten times worse. But if he did help them – if he did do his part of the swear – his father would be really chuffed for once. Oh it wasn't *fair*.

The idea of running away came back to him. Why not *now*, though? Why not leave the bedroom now, and go to kill the soldier? If his mother found out, she would kill him – but that might be ages. By then – who knew? They might have . . . they might be . . . heroes!

Thomas, filled with excitement, got carefully off the bed. This time, there would be no mistakes and no noise. No matches, either; but . . .

He thought of Sarah, and of what he had told his mother. But she had not left the house, so . . . And in any case, if he was quick . . . He took a deep breath and tiptoed to the bedroom door.

If he was quick it would still be all right.

Everything . . .

Sarah set a cracking pace, and she was furious. Thomas, trying to carry the milk jug and keep up, was whining at her.

'Slow down,' he fretted. 'I'm spilling it, slow down.'

'We can't slow down,' said Sarah, over her shoulder. 'There isn't time, we're late already.'

'Fat lot of good it'll be if there's no milk when we get there,' said Thomas. 'Fat lot of good tea is with no milk.'

Sarah said bitterly: 'Fat lot of good tea is without a fire, Dumbo. We might as well give up before we start. One piddling little thing we ask you to get and you don't. A little thing like matches. *And* it was you who said you had some. You little liar.'

'I'm *not* a liar,' Thomas panted. 'She must have taken them, my Mum. She must have found them in my drawer. *Honestly.*'

'Yah, you're full of excuses you are, Thomas Wyatt,' Sarah replied. 'You're useless. Come on, lift your feet up.'

Another big white slurp of milk escaped over the rim of the jug onto the windblown grass. Thomas stopped.

'What's the hurry, anyway?' he demanded. 'Sarah, I'm *spilling* it.'

Sarah walked back and looked into the jug. She sighed.

'The hurry is,' she said, taking his arm and pushing him forward, 'because we haven't got much time. Before much longer, Thomas, there'll be soldiers everywhere. That raid last night, the battle. There was lots and lots of damage, shot down planes and things. There'll be soldiers everywhere, looking for stragglers and that. My Mum didn't really want to let me out, she was dead against it.' She pushed him harder. 'And then you go and hold us up, and you haven't even got the matches. I don't know!'

Thomas moved faster, but he was on the verge of sulking.

'What does it matter, though?' he said. 'Why the heck should we care if he's cold or not, or has a cup of tea? We're only going to kill him. Get it over with, I say.'

Sarah was already several feet ahead.

'Don't be so bloody daft, kid,' she replied. 'Just lift your feet up and shift.'

Thomas stopped so suddenly that he spilled a lot more milk.

'What do you mean "don't be so bloody daft"?' he said. 'Are you saying we're *not* going to kill him now? Are you—'

Sarah sprang angrily to save the milk. Thomas slipped, the jug fell. It rolled, empty, on the grass. She looked at him in disgust.

'Oh God, Thomas,' she said, 'I just don't know about you. Look, how do you think we're going to do it, then? Poison him? Set fire to the hut? He's got a gun, you fool. He's got a ruddy *rifle*. He's a *soldier*.'

Thomas said eagerly: 'But it's all worked out! We'll lull him into a sense of false se . . thingity. We'll give him tea and blankets. We'll make him go to sleep. And then . . . and then . . .' His eagerness began to fade. 'We'll drop a rock on him. Michael said so.

74

We'll smash his head in. He's got it all worked out . . .'

Sarah put the jug on to a large rock, where they could find it later. She hoicked the blanket firmly over her shoulder, handing the sandwiches to Thomas.

'Come on, you take these. We'll leave the jug, it's pointless empty. We've got to run.'

Thomas still hung back.

'But we've *got* to kill him,' he told Sarah. 'We swore an oath. We'll make him warm and comfortable and then we'll smash his head in. Michael said so.'

Sarah started to walk, briskly.

'You're disgusting, you are. That would be cold blood. Murder in cold blood. I sometimes wonder if you're thick or not, Thomas Wyatt. Michael's a little monster.'

Thomas had to tag along; he *had* to work this out.

'But *he's* a murderer,' he said pathetically. '*He's* killed British soldiers in cold blood. It's him who's a monster, not us. We swore an oath.'

'Listen, Thomas,' Sarah said. 'I'm not angry, honestly, but you *must* hurry up. Look, you're just a kid, right? You don't understand. Michael is a nutcase. It's all a silly game. No one's killing anyone, got it? Nobody. We've got to save this soldier, nothing else. He's cold and hungry and wounded. We've got to save his life. Now *move*.'

'*Save* him?' he said. 'But we can't! We can't! Sarah. We *can't* save his life . . .'

It felt to Michael as if he had been looking down the rifle-barrel at the soldier's face for a lifetime. It felt as if his finger on the trigger would break with tension. Bone of skull, brown, dirty, stubble-covered cheek, the eyes closed and, underneath the eyelids, trembling. The first pressure on the trigger had been easy. But his finger, aching and bent, was paralysed.

75

'You're the enemy,' Michael whispered. And the eyes, beneath the grey, exhausted eyelids, fluttered.

When they opened, it took them several seconds to focus on Michael's own. Michael could not even blink. They stared at each other for a long long moment, neither moving nor speaking.

Then, very slowly, Michael took his finger from the trigger, and his hand from the stock. The rifle was heavy, his arms ached. He held it in his left hand, then bent his knees and placed it on the ground. He stood up.

Unsmiling, and in a dry and croaking voice, the soldier asked him: 'Why did you not? Boy? Why did you not?'

Rage and shame filled Michael. He had failed. He turned away racked with anger and self-disgust. He hated the soldier, lying there, grey-faced and despairing, he hated him enough to . . .

Michael turned back to the young man on the ground. He clenched his fists.

'It's not *fair*,' he shouted. 'We swore an oath. To do it *together*. I can't kill you on my own, it's not fair on the *others*.'

The soldier stared at him, uncomprehending.

'You wouldn't understand, you sod,' Michael went on. 'You wouldn't understand. It's honour, see? *We're* not savages. You wouldn't *understand*.'

The soldier's face was sad, immobile. He moved his head slightly. Michael saw that his eyes were full of tears.

The soldier said: 'Help me. Please. I am very cold. Help me.'

Chapter Ten

It took Sarah ages to find out just what was up with Thomas, but she got there in the end. The last time she had left him, to hurry on, Thomas had not followed. After walking for a while, she had turned round, expecting him to be there. But he was lying on a grassy knoll, his head covered by his arms.

'Thomas,' she shrieked. 'Come on! You've got the sandwiches!'

He had not come, and she had gone back. Her anger evaporated when she saw his face. He looked terror-stricken.

'What's up, Tom?' she asked. 'Now what is it? Look, we've got to hurry, don't you understand?'

'*You* don't understand,' said Thomas. 'We've got to kill him because I ran away. My Mum caught me with the matches, she found me. They were in my hand, in my bedroom, they were all over the floor.'

'You poor thing,' said Sarah. 'You must have been scared. But never mind the matches, that's just too bad. Let's *shift*, Thomas.'

He flashed a look of temper at her.

'You idiot,' he snapped. 'I ran *away*. She told me I was to stay there till my Dad came back. And I didn't. I ran away to you. So we've got to kill the soldier or they'll kill me. It's our patriotic duty. Even my Dad won't mind if I do something like that. Otherwise I . . . Sarah, I ran *away*.'

Sarah was sympathetic, but she was also dead worried. If Mrs Wyatt had spoken to Thomas, questioned him . . . She took his wrist.

'Look, Thomas,' she said. 'Answer me something straight. Dead straight. What did you tell your mother? About why you wanted matches? What did you say?'

The speed of Thomas's answer made her stomach sink.

'Nothing! I didn't tell her nothing! I said . . . I said . . .'

'Yes? You said what?'

'I said we . . . I said . . .' His face cleared. He'd had an idea. 'I didn't say anything. I ran away!'

'You did *not* run straight away,' said Sarah sternly. 'Because, remember, your mother told you to wait for your Dad. Tell me the truth, Thomas. It's *urgent*.'

Thomas stuck his lower lip out.

'You can't make me,' he muttered. 'Anyway—'

Sarah lost her rag. She threw the blanket and stuff to the ground and seized him roughly by the arm. She made a fist and held it in his face.

'You told her, didn't you? You told her!'

Thomas caved in. He began to whimper.

'She didn't believe me, Sarah! I swear it! I said it was a game!'

Sarah let her fist drop to her side. She was limp, the fury drained away.

'You told her there was a soldier, injured on the moors. Oh my God.'

Thomas was ashamed.

'I said it was pretend, Sarah. I swear it, I swear. She didn't believe me, *honestly*.'

Sarah was no longer facing him.

'You gutless little sod, Thomas,' she said flatly. 'You gutless little swine.'

'But I'm *here*,' squawked Thomas, appalled by the unfairness of this. Would *she* dare to disobey an order? 'I'm here, so how can I be gutless? I ran away from *Mum*!'

Sarah was sunk in gloom.

'And where's your Dad?' she muttered. 'Oh God. Oh never mind. Oh glory hallelujah.'

Thomas whispered. 'I only did it 'cause we're going to kill him. Honestly. I ran away from *Mum*.'

In her kitchen, Mrs Wyatt stared into a cupboard. Two shotguns were leaning against the wall, and she had a box of cartridges in her hand, half open.

'He's such a terrible little liar,' she said. 'It's just a stupid lie.'

She pulled a cartridge from the box and tapped her teeth with it. She wondered whether to go and question Thomas some more.

'No, he'll want that,' she decided. 'He'd like to have a chat. I'll leave him stewing in his juice.'

She pushed the cartridge back among the others, but she put them on the kitchen table, not into the cupboard.

'I'll wait until his Dad gets home,' she said.

In the shelter, Michael had managed to make the soldier comfortable. He had helped him to a wall where the sun still reached, he had pulled him up until his back was straight, and he had wrapped his clothes around him to give him the best possible protection from the chilling draughts that got in through the broken walls.

Best of all, Michael had lit a fire. For the soldier, in a tin that smelled of tobacco, had had some matches. He had rattled the tin feebly, until Michael had caught on, and opened it.

'Empty,' he said, disappointed. 'You want to smoke? No cigarettes.'

The soldier had smiled, a painful smile. He had shaken his head.

'Flames,' he said. 'Warm. Flames.'

'Oh,' said Michael. 'Yeah! Great! I'll light a fire.'

Gathering small wood had taken a good few minutes, then he had broken off some bigger pieces from the old roof timbers. Every time he had caught the soldier's eye, they had smiled at each other, and nodded. 'Good', and 'Good boy' would say the soldier. 'Yeah', and 'Great' Michael would reply.

Then a handful of dried grass from the corner, and the flames had taken. Michael had worried momentarily about the smoke, but what could he do? Anyway, he'd gone outside and looked, and there was nothing visible, nothing to give them away. The keen strong wind blew the smoke to nothing very quickly.

When the fire was going well, they had tried to have a conversation. But it was not much good. Although the soldier was not in agony at the moment, as far as Michael could tell, he could hardly speak a word in English. At times, even 'good boy' was too much for him. Of his language, Michael knew nothing.

Then, with a sudden smile, the soldier patted his combat jacket pocket. Slowly, he reached into it. Slowly he pulled out his cassette recorder. Still smiling, he offered it to Michael.

'Is ma . . . is mother,' he said, quietly. 'She say . . . she say, when come home.'

Michael, prepared, did not expect to hear pop music. But on the tape there were snatches of music, and many different voices. The word 'Maria' occurred a lot.

After a short while, the sound distorted slightly. He switched the cassette off quickly. The batteries sounded weak. He smiled.

'Maria?' he asked. 'Is that your mother, then? Or your . . .?'

The soldier shook his head, slowly. He pointed to his chest.

80

'Maria,' he said. 'My is Maria. You?'

'Oh,' said Michael, surprised. 'Me Michael. I—'

Like an echo, his name sounded again. Michael jumped.

'Crikey!' he said. 'It must be Sarah and Thomas. Hang on a second.'

It was too late for him to pretend he had been keeping guard. Sarah came straight in with the blanket, the kettle and the water bottle, and he did not dare to tell her off for approaching so carelessly. Thomas slunk in a second later. He went and sat in the shadow in the corner.

'Quick,' said Sarah. 'We've got some food. Oh! You've got a fire going!'

'Yeah,' said Michael. 'He had some matches in a tin.'

He was feeling nervous, and ashamed again. He did not know how Sarah would react to what had happened. She was looking round, staring at the soldier, staring at everything.

Michael said: 'Look, Sarah. I'm sorry. I got his gun all right, but I . . . well I . . . Look, I couldn't kill him.'

Sarah gave him an odd look and laughed.

'Of course you couldn't, you fool,' she said. She held out the blanket. 'Just get this round his legs while I put the kettle on. Of course you couldn't kill him.'

Michael took the blanket, but he did not unfold it.

'You understand?' he said. 'You're not . . .?'

'Oh get the blanket down,' said Sarah. She poured some water into the kettle, then placed it carefully in the fire. 'I've got some sandwiches as well, but no milk. Thomas had to spill it, didn't he?'

She glared at Thomas in his corner, and added with heavy sarcasm: 'Oh yes, we understand, don't we, Thomas? We understand perfectly.'

Michael looked from one of them to the other. He opened out the blanket.

81

'I don't know what you mean,' he said. 'And I don't know what's going on. What's up with *him*?'

Sarah rubbed her forehead with the back of her hand. She noticed the water bottle top in it, and put it in her pocket.

'He's told,' she said. 'That's what's the matter, Michael. He's told his rotten mother.'

Mrs Wyatt decided to have another word with Thomas when she saw her husband's Land Rover crossing the field towards the back gate. She opened his bedroom door quietly, in case he'd gone to sleep. When she discovered he had run, she was filled with anger. Then with fear.

Her husband would hardly believe it as she blurted out her story. But as he questioned her, he loaded both the shotguns and filled his pockets with cartridges.

'There's Army all around,' he said. 'They're crawling about all over the place. If they come here before I meet them tell them what you know. Either way we'll—'

He pushed a shotgun into his wife's hands.

'Up that way then, you reckon? Is that the way they play? Oh, if I catch that little devil first I'll . . .'

'Be careful with him, Jim,' his wife said. 'Don't go crazy with him.'

Mr Wyatt looked at her coldly.

'I'll slaughter him,' he said. 'If he comes back, hide him, that's all. Keep him from my sight.'

Chapter Eleven

Normally, Michael would probably have done something to Thomas, but this time he was at a loss. He glanced into the shadow, then at Sarah. Sarah shrugged.

'What can you say?' she said. 'I nearly killed him when he told me, but what can you say?'

'But . . . but. He's *told*? What does that . . .? I mean? Hell, Sarah! What are we going to do?'

Sarah walked over to Thomas and took the sandwiches from him. She rapidly opened the paper. She approached the soldier, shyly. He looked ill, and agonized, but he tried to smile at her.

Sarah handed a single sandwich to him, and the soldier took it. She noticed that his hand was filthy, and that it was shaking.

'Here, Mister,' she said. 'Eat some food.' She smiled, politely. 'It's corned beef. You'll like that, won't you?'

Sickly, the soldier returned the smile. He slowly raised the sandwich to his mouth, and when it was there, he parted his lips. Hardly wide enough, however, for the sandwich to go in. He pressed the bread against his lips, until he could bite. Sarah, embarassed, turned away.

'Thank you,' the soldier said. 'Good children. Thank you.'

Sarah turned back to him. The sandwich, hardly touched, was by his mouth. His eyes were intensely brown. She could not look at him. Seeing her expression, the soldier moved the sandwich to his mouth once more.

'Your friend,' he whispered. He moved his eyes to indicate Michael. 'Your friend. Good boy.'

Then, as if to please her, to reassure her, he opened his mouth wider. He slowly bit the sandwich.

'Sarah?' said Michael.

'He says his mother doesn't believe him,' said Sarah. She walked rapidly from the soldier, left him to try and eat. She wondered if she should break the meat up, what she should do. Easier to talk to Michael.

'He says she doesn't, but it's not the point. He says he ran away, she sent him to his room. When she finds out he's gone, that's that. Michael, they'll be looking soon, they're bound to be. We've got to save him, Michael.'

'Who'll be looking? Mr Wyatt and his friends? Thomas's D—'

'Ssh.'

But Thomas was not listening. Fascinated, he was watching the soldier. He could not eat, Thomas could tell. He could not get his mouth to work. Slowly, Thomas moved towards him. He held his hand out.

'Here,' said Thomas. 'Give it over. I'll get the meat out for you.'

The soldier did not understand, but he gave the sandwich up. Thomas separated the bread quickly, and pulled out a small lump of beef. He put it between the soldier's lips. The man began to chew.

'There,' said Thomas. 'Finish that and I'll give you a drink of water. Until your tea gets made.'

The soldier, painfully, swallowed. He parted his lips for more.

'The Army'd be all right,' Sarah was saying. 'They've got rules. They'd make him into a prisoner. But if Gregory and his gang . . . You know, hotheads. Well.'

Michael made sure his voice was low.

'You don't think they'd actually . .? You know. You

84

don't believe they really . .? Over at Foster's Landing? When they found those others? You know . . . killed . . .?'

Sarah shook her head.

'Ssh,' went Sarah. 'Look, Michael, no I don't. People don't really *do* things like . . . But they might be . . . angry, you know. Cruel. I mean if Tommy's Dad thought— If *your* Dad, even . . .'

She stopped. Michael, without meaning to, caught her eye.

'If *your* Dad,' he breathed. 'If he thought you were in danger. If he—'

Sarah interrupted him, her voice quite loud.

'We've got to get him somewhere safe,' she said. 'Soldiers or whatever, he's just a boy, Michael, on his own. We've got to—'

'Soldiers? You talk soldiers?'

They both jumped. The soldier's eyes were on them. Thomas was beside him, the cassette-player headphones in his hand.

'No,' he murmured. 'No tell the Army. Please. No tell the Army.'

Michael tried to sound jovial. He made a gesture with his hand.

'All right, Maria,' he said loudly. 'You'll be all right. Don't you worry, eat your sandwiches.'

The soldier did not eat. He stared at them.

'Maria?' said Sarah.

'That's his name,' said Michael. Then he added, uncertainly: 'I think.'

Thomas got up off his knees.

'But that's a girl's name,' he said.

'Oh shut up, Tom,' said Michael tiredly. 'Look, come outside the pair of you. Quickly. We've got to talk.'

Mr Wyatt drove the Land Rover through the stream so

fast that water sprayed over the windscreen. He cursed as the vehicle jerked sideways and he slid bodily across the seat.

'Wounded soldier on the moor,' he muttered. 'If he's telling stories I'll—'

He double-declutched and revved hard to slam the engine into a lower gear. As he bounced round a bend in the track he saw movement ahead.

'Aha,' he said. He reached for the horn button. 'At long bloody last.'

Michael and Thomas and Sarah looked down the long moor. The sun was past its best now, and there were huge cloud shadows racing across the grass. Outside the shelter, it was getting very cold. Michael pointed the stick he was carrying at Thomas's chest.

'Remember, Thomas,' he said. 'One more chance. Go down to the bottom, and watch. If you see anyone moving, *anyone*, get back here.'

He stabbed with the staff. Thomas flinched.

'And Thomas. If there *is* anyone, no matter who, don't let them see which way you go. Get back up here fast, and don't be seen, got it? Under any circumstances.'

Thomas nodded.

'If you let us down once more,' Michael finished, 'you're for it. Understand?'

Thomas did. Michael took his shoulder, and shoved it hard. He jumped onto the first hummock, got his balance, and fled. Michael and Sarah watched him running down the moor.

'Right,' said Michael. 'Let's try and move him. Let's see if we can get Maria shifted.'

But the soldier was in the middle of a wave of agony. They got him halfway to his feet, the blanket round his shoulders, but they could see it was no good. His face was pale and washed with a freezing sweat. Each time he tried to put weight on his legs he almost passed out. A low, frightening noise came constantly from his throat.

'You've got to move, you've *got* to,' said Sarah. 'We've got to hide you from the men.'

'We've got to hide him from bloody Thomas,' said Michael. 'Thomas and his great big mouth.'

The soldier sagged down. They could hardly hold his weight.

'Soldiers come?' he croaked. 'Not tell soldiers?'

'Not the soldiers, no,' said Sarah, urgently. 'It's farmers. They're angry. They have guns. The soldiers are all right. We've got to hide you from the men.'

The soldier, nearly upright, put weight onto his left leg. He made a sharp groaning noise, a swallowed scream. He doubled over.

'No. Hurting. Ah. Hurting.'

The children, distraught, supported him as he sank downwards. His face was awful.

'Lie back, lie back,' said Sarah. 'Oh Michael, he's in agony.'

'Yeah,' said Michael. He helped the soldier to support himself against the wall, not far from the inner entrance. Together, they spread the blanket loosely over his legs.

'Come on, Maria,' said Michael. 'You lie back. You're not going anywhere. Lie back.'

Thomas, over the brow of the next low hill, kept looking back, although he knew he could not see the shelter. He wished he could, he missed the sight of it, he was lonely.

'I don't think it's fair,' he said out loud. 'What am I meant to be here for? Why couldn't I stay with them? It's stupid.'

He was bending for a rock to chuck when he heard a noise above the wind. A new noise. He stood upright and scanned the horizon.

As the wind bustled round the moorland the noise came louder.

It was an engine.

Sarah, by the outer wall, was looking down the moor also. She had left the soldier because she could hardly bear to look at him. She was desperately afraid, now. Afraid of what might happen.

As Michael joined her, she said. 'Michael. We've got to call the soldiers in. It's the only hope. They'll give him drugs and stuff. He'll be a prisoner of war. They'll put him on a stretcher in a helicopter. It's the only hope.'

'But he's terrified of them,' Michael replied. 'I know it's stupid, but he's petrified. It's propaganda, I suppose. He must believe the British Army are . . . well, it's crazy.'

He paused.

'It *is* crazy,' he went on, 'isn't it? We're scared of the farmers, and he's scared of the soldiers. And we'll both be wrong, I bet. It's stupid, stupid, stupid. It's games, Sarah, just games. Like us . . . like me thinking we could . . . I could . . . you know.'

Before Sarah could reply, she saw the bobble-hat, and then the face, of Thomas. He burst over the brow of the hill, running hard.

'Oh Michael! There's Thomas! The farmers must be—Oh my God, oh no!'

But before Thomas was fully over the top, a helicopter rose into view behind him. The sound of it, battling the strong wind, reached them a second later. From where they were, it looked as if it was almost on him, as if it were attacking him like an enormous dragonfly. They could see his arms waving, they could see his mouth shouting as the machine passed over him, and thudded its way towards them.

'The Army,' Michael said. He said it softly. 'Thank God for that. They've got here first.'

Sarah and Michael turned to each other, with smiles upon their faces. Smiles of huge relief.

From inside the shelter, the voice of the soldier came to them. It was hoarse with fear.

'Soldiers? Not tell soldiers! They kill! They kill!'

Sarah ran to the doorway. She hardly noticed that the soldier was on his knees, holding his rifle like a crutch, trying to stand. She shouted joyfully, above the growing noise of the helicopter: 'No! They'll save you! The British are coming. Good men! Good! They'll save you.'

As she rejoined Michael, a stream of men in combat gear appeared at the top of the hill. They spread across the horizon, then followed the helicopter. They ran crouched down, they held rifles at the ready by their sides, they had darkened faces and wore berets. A new fear seized both of them at once. It was a fearsome sight.

'We'd better go and warn them, though,' said Michael. 'We'd better just explain.'

Thomas, racing and careering towards them, was still waving his arms and shouting. Still the helicopter's beating roar drowned everything. Sarah and Michael, white-faced, suddenly began to run towards him, towards the helicopter, towards the stream of men. As they ran, they saw Thomas fall, and the soldiers pass him.

Sarah opened her mouth to shout, but the helicopter was overhead. It was as if its sound were battering her, it was appalling. She could see the men close-to now, their anxious, urgent faces.

'He's a boy,' screamed Michael. 'He's harmless! He's just a boy!'

The men were bursting past them, an unstoppable tide. Sarah tried to seize one, but was brushed aside. Their eyes were fixed, intent.

She screamed into the thunder: 'He's badly hurt! A prisoner! He needs your help!'

Then Michael and Sarah appeared to be alone, cocooned in noise and terror. The helicopter and the men had passed them by.

And as Thomas reached them, screaming loudly, piercingly loudly, hysterically, they heard the shots.

A burst, or flurry. The clipped, sharp bark of rifles.

Then, as they all three watched in utter silence, the helicopter landed.

Chapter Twelve

That night there were no sounds of war, but only Thomas slept. He slept after he had cried himself exhausted, and Red Bear's fur was soaked. He had a sore bottom and legs from where his father had punished him, and he dreamed his awful dream. It awoke him twice, tense with horror, and each time, he cried himself to sleep again. Thinking of the soldier, and of giving him a drink, and of feeding him little bits of corned beef from the sandwiches.

Michael lay on his back for endless hours, holding his knife on his stomach as a comforter. He felt sick and stunned with the shock of it all, but with little twinges of excitement, despite himself. The men and the helicopter had been terrifying, true – but marvellous, as well. The noise, the urgency, the . . . then he would remember Maria, and the shots. Then he would squirm, and twist, and worry.

What had his father said? It served the bugger right. Of course it served him right. He was a soldier, fighting in a war, and he got what was coming to him. Michael had tried to explain that it had not been like that, but his father had laughed.

'He was there, so he bought it,' he said. 'What did you expect them to do – give him a kiss or something? You know what they say, Mike. All's fair in love and war.'

But he was injured, thought Michael. He was ill. He was a prisoner of war. Well – he should have been. What had gone wrong? Surely that was not what *should* have happened? Surely there were rules?

Sarah lay between her parents in their bed, and for once they told her things. Hard things, nasty things. She had told them everything, and she had asked them why.

'Look, Sarah-love,' said Dad, when they had heard it all three times at least. 'There could be lots of ways it happened, and lots of reasons. It could have been an accident, it could have been deliberate, it could have been—'

'How, an accident?' asked Sarah. 'He was hurt. He could hardly move. He needed help.'

'He had a rifle,' her mother said.

'Yes, he used it as a crutch. He was—'

'Listen, Bum,' said Dad. 'We can only tell you what might have happened. You'll have to make your own mind up in the end, you know. Do you want to hear?'

Sarah wanted to hear. She wanted to talk. She wanted to be with them, awake, whatever happened. Her father pointed out that the soldiers could have been afraid, that they could have been confused, that they could even have been fired on.

'But—'

'Did you see the shooting?'

'Well no, but—'

'But nothing, Sarah. Those are just the things that might have happened. Those men might have gone up to the doorway, and he might have been sitting there, even in the state you say he was in, and he might have shot at them.'

Sarah turned this over and over in her mind. The soldier shoot at *them*?

As if reading her thoughts, her mother said: 'That's what he was there for, after all.'

'But do you believe it?' Sarah asked.

Her father's laugh rumbled in the darkened bedroom.

'You were there, my love,' he said. 'We weren't. Practically anything can happen in war, I do believe that. As for the rest. Well . . . you were there.'

Sarah buried her face in her mother's nightie then, to try to blot out images. She knew what she believed.

Up on the freezing moor, pressed into the mud of the shelter floor by a soldier's boot, the cassette-player lay silently.

There was a scrap of scarf nearby it, fluttering in the wind, and three slices of bread and butter. In the ashes of the fire lay the remains of the kettle, melted and black.

But the soldier's remains were gone.

Albeson and the Germans

JAN NEEDLE

It seems a very simple thing that starts off all the trouble — a rumour that two German children are coming to Church Street School. Although the teachers cannot understand the panic that this causes, Albeson can. His comics, and his dead grandfather have taught him all about Germans. And he doesn't fancy the idea one little bit.

The plan that Albeson's friend Pam comes up with frightens him stiff. Unfortunately, his mate Smithie, who's very tough and sometimes a bit odd, likes the idea. So Albeson has no choice. From then on, everything Albeson does gets him deeper and deeper into trouble, and finally, danger.

'Gripping, lively and funny — It really grabs you'

Daily Mirror

THE CHRONICLES OF PRYDAIN

Lloyd Alexander

Taran, the assistant pig-keeper, is only too glad of a long-awaited opportunity to seek adventure and heroism. But he and his odd assortment of faithful companions become involved in a life-and-death struggle against the evil Horned King of Annuvin, Land of the Dead, and his dark forces which threaten to overrun the land of Prydain. It is a far-reaching struggle, lasting many years and involving folk and creatures from every kingdom of Prydain.

In his very popular series of five novels, Lloyd Alexander combines elements of myth and Welsh legend with high adventure and humour to create a strange, coherent and richly satisfying world of his own which will appeal especially to Tolkien and Narnia addicts. Though each of the five books, listed below, can be read separately, they form a sequence culminating in *The High King*, for which the author won the coveted Newbery Medal.

'The strongest fantasy being created for children in our time.' *School Library Journal*

'Immensely worth discovering.' *The Observer*

The Chronicles of Prydain are all available in Lions:

The Book of Three; The Black Cauldron; The Castle of Llyr; Taran Wanderer; The High King.

The Third Class Genie

ROBERT LEESON

Disasters were leading two nil on Alec's disaster-triumph scorecard, when he slipped into the vacant factory lot, locally known as the Tank. Ginger Wallace was hot on his heels, ready to destroy him, and Alec had escaped just in the nick of time. There were disasters awaiting him at home too, when he discovered that he would have to move out of his room and into the boxroom. And, of course, there was school . . .

But Alec's luck changed when he found a beer can that was still sealed, but obviously empty. Stranger still, when he held it up to his ear, he could hear a faint snoring . . . When Alec finally opened the mysterious can, something happened that gave triumphs a roaring and most unexpected lead.

A hilarious story for readers of ten upwards.